www.marvel.com

TM & © 2012 Marvel & Subs.

Published by Marvel Press, an imprint of Disney Book Group. No part of this book may be reproduced or transmitted in any form or by any means, electronic or mechanical, including photocopying, recording, or by any information storage and retrieval system, without written permission from the publisher. For information address Marvel Press, 114 Fifth Avenue, New York, New York 10011-5690.

Jacket and Case Illustrated by Pat Olliffe and Brian Miller
Designed by Jason Wojtowicz

Printed in the United States of America
First Edition
1 3 5 7 9 10 8 6 4 2
G942-9090-6-12032
ISBN 978-1-4231-6032-8

SUSTAINABLE FORESTRY INITIATIVE

Certified Sourcing
www.sfiprogram.org

In this place, the earth is frozen and the water is ice.
The shoreline is like a wall between two worlds—
the sea and the land.

Both are silent and still.

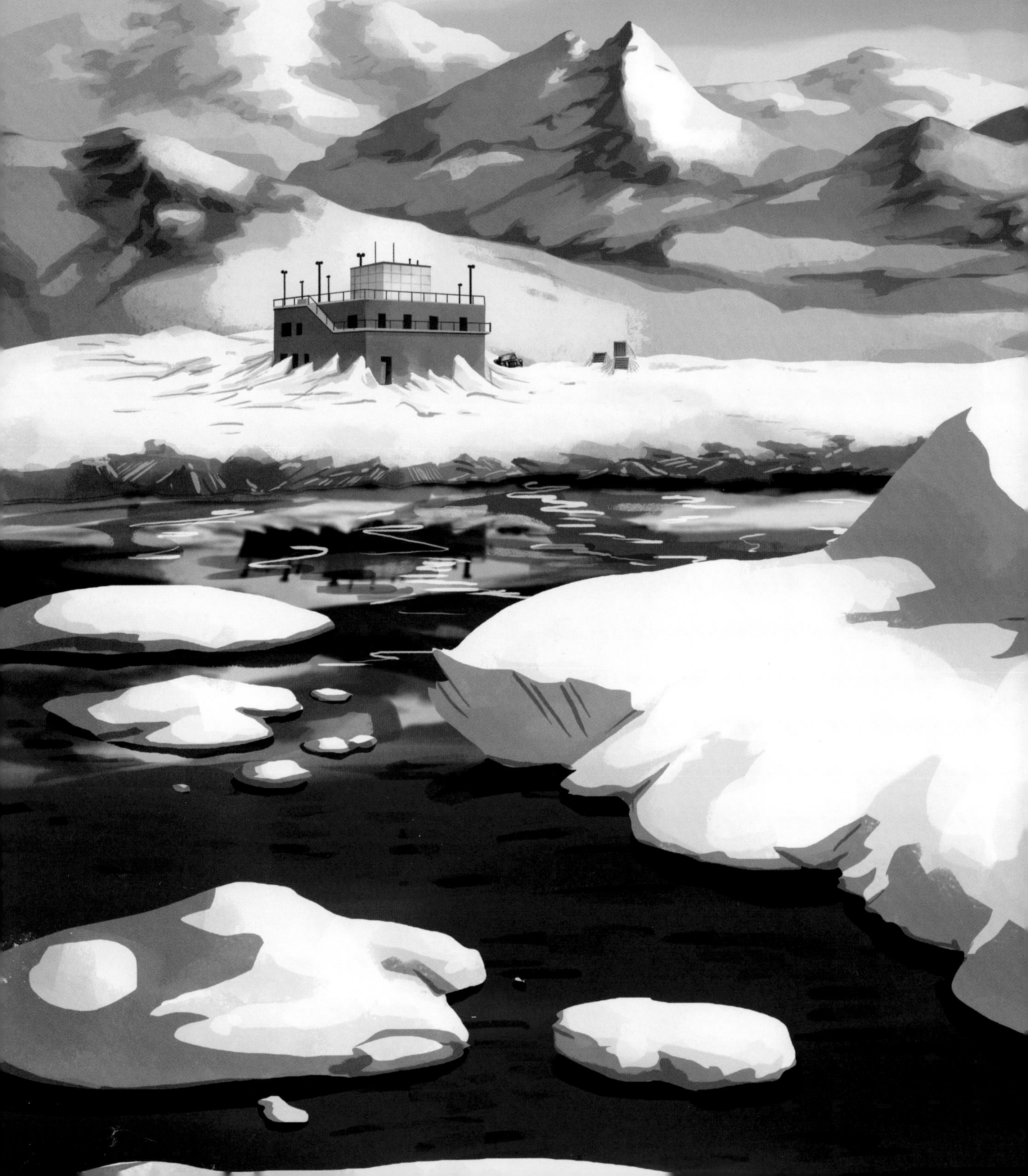

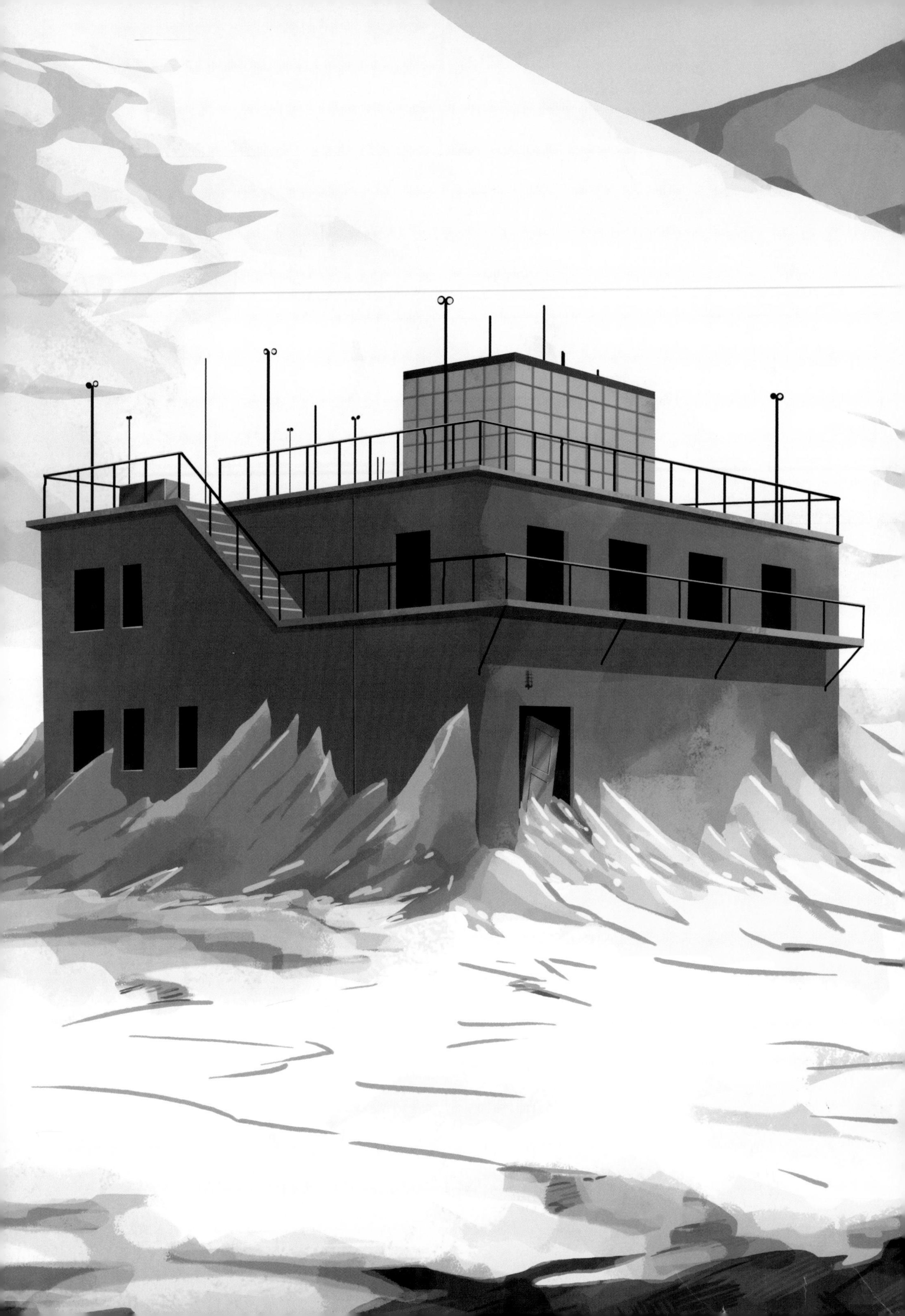

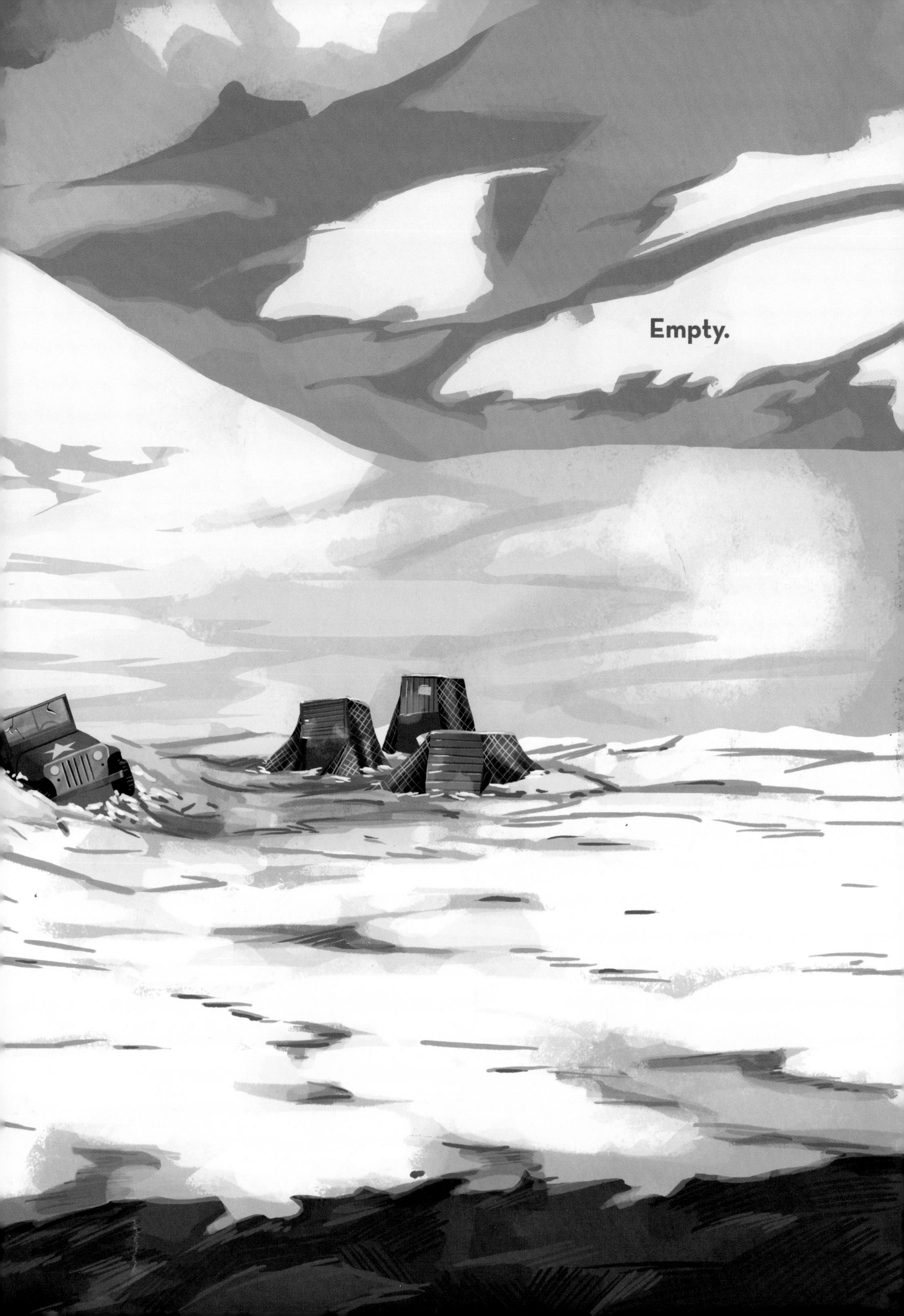

Empty.

But this was not always so.

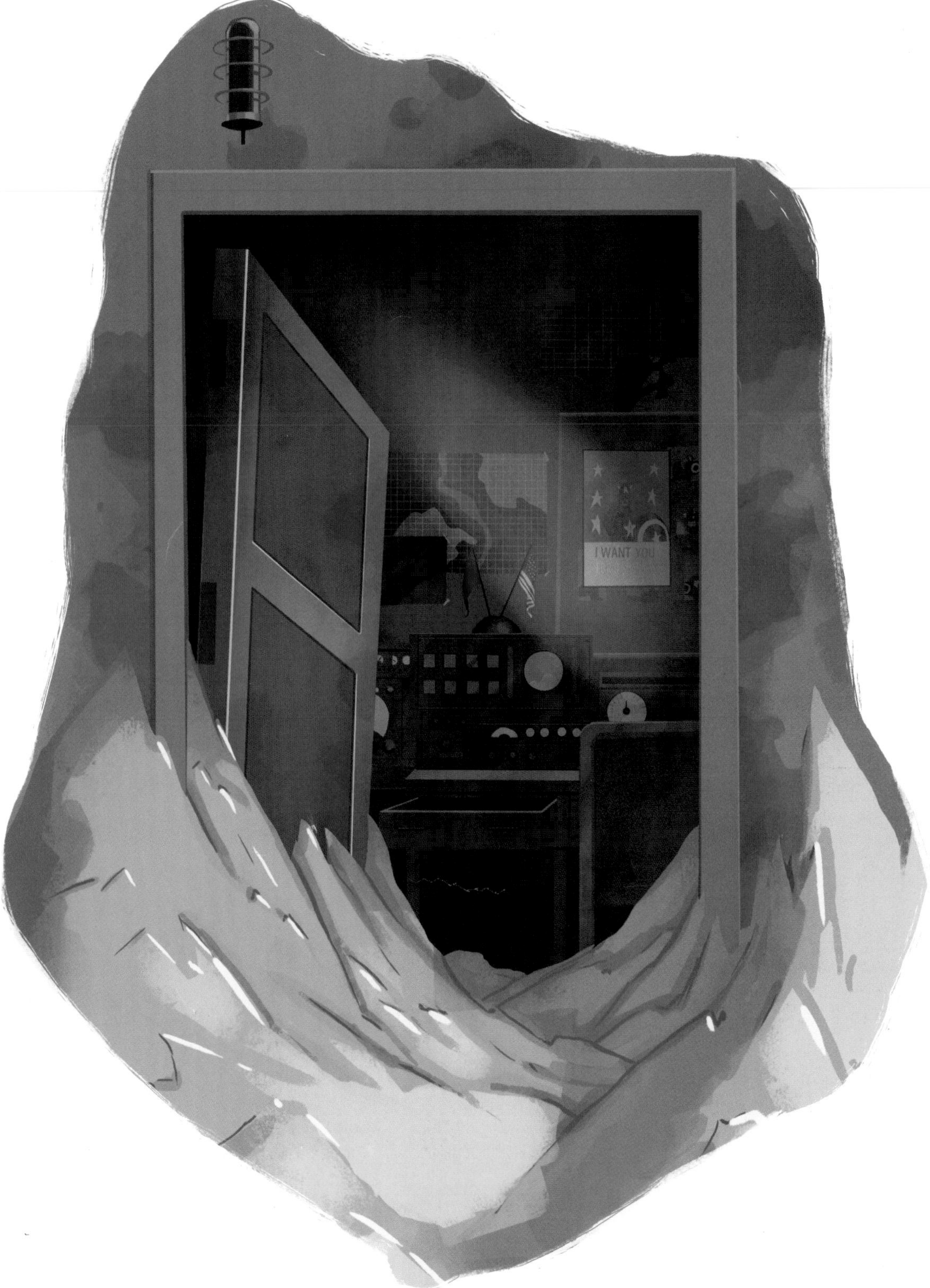
I WANT YOU

Long ago, soldiers stood watch here.

They fought in terrible wars,
but they did not fight alone.

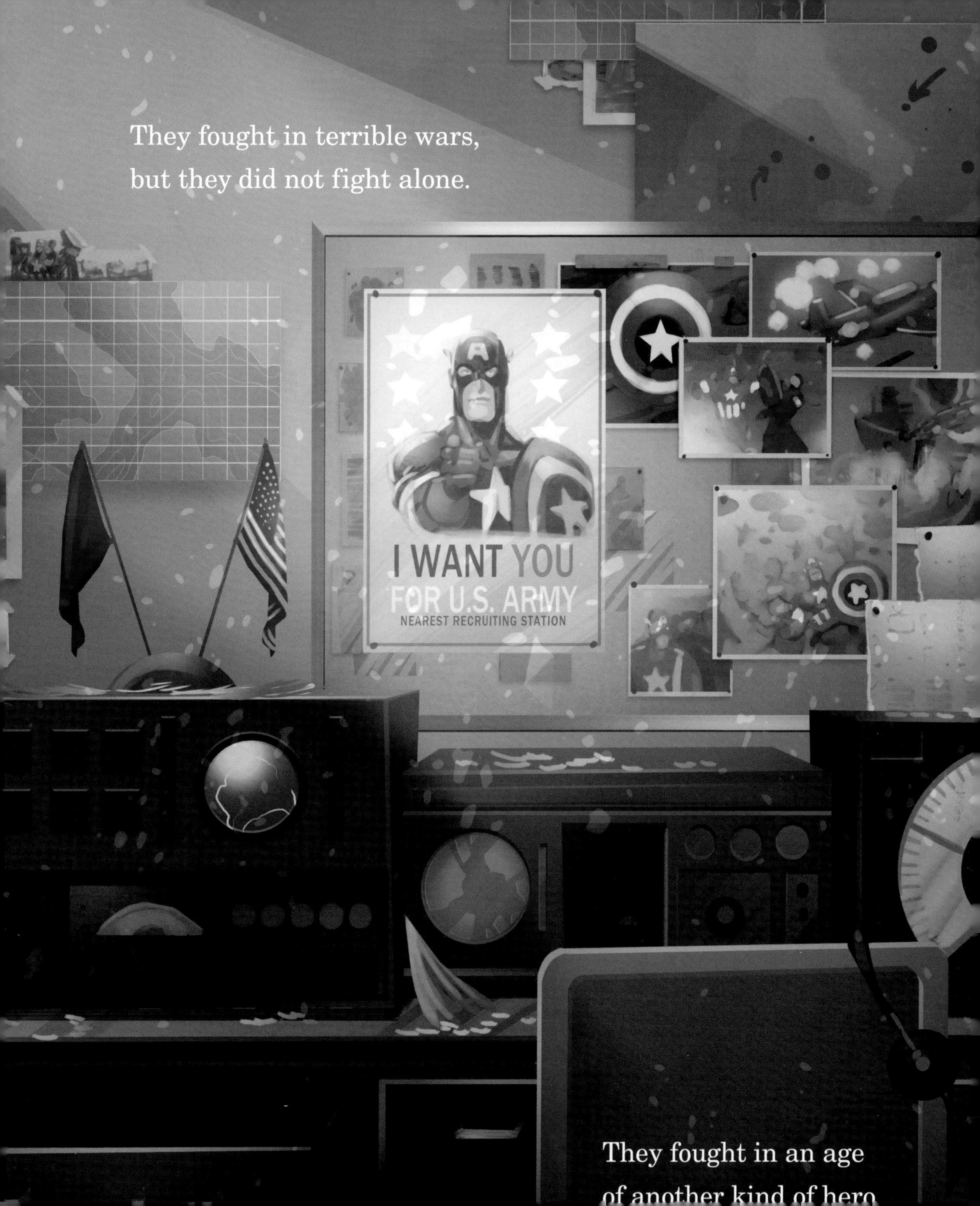
I WANT YOU
FOR U.S. ARMY
NEAREST RECRUITING STATION

They fought in an age
of another kind of hero

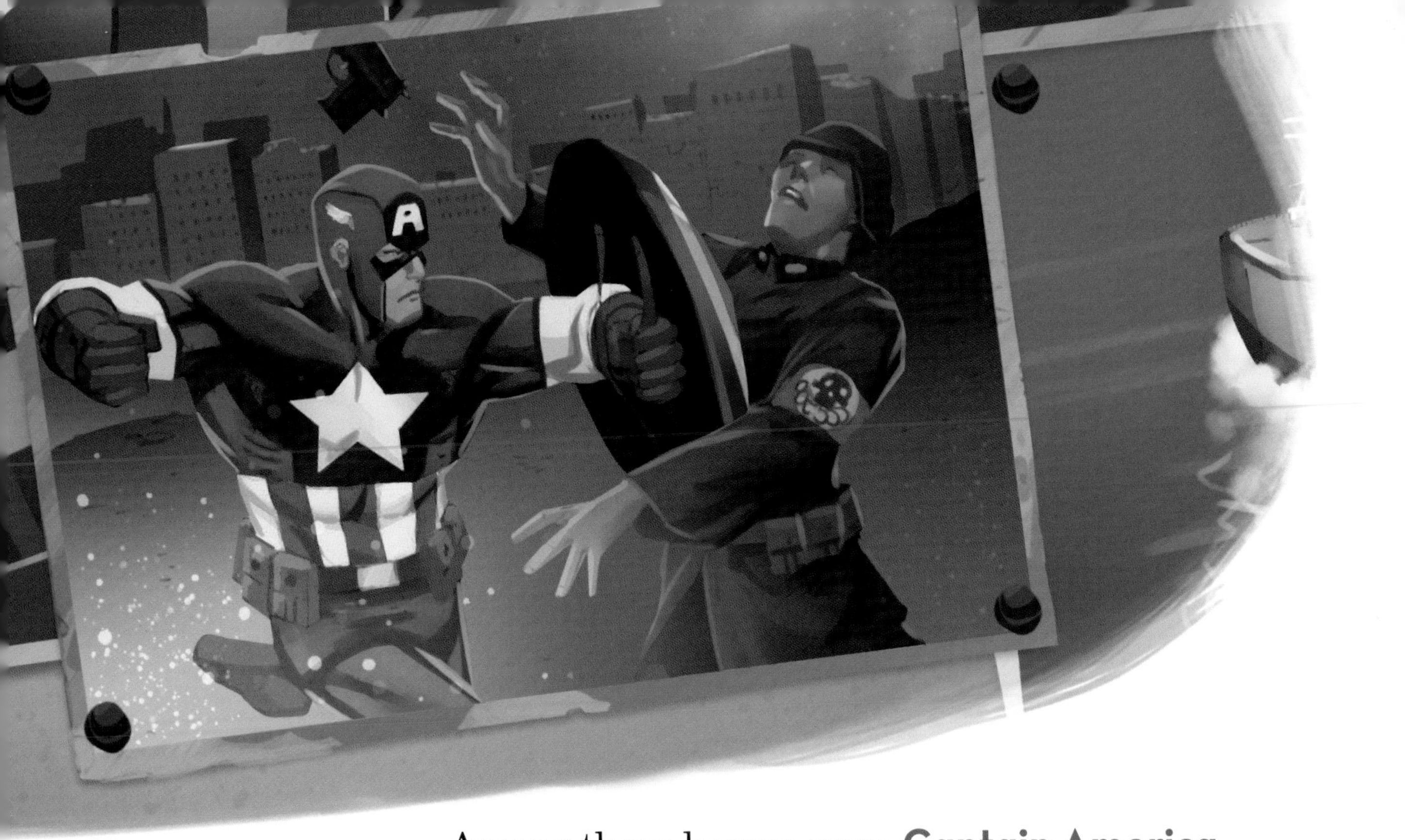

Among these heroes were **Captain America**—
Super-Soldier and defender of freedom—

and **Namor**, prince of the undersea
kingdom Atlantis.

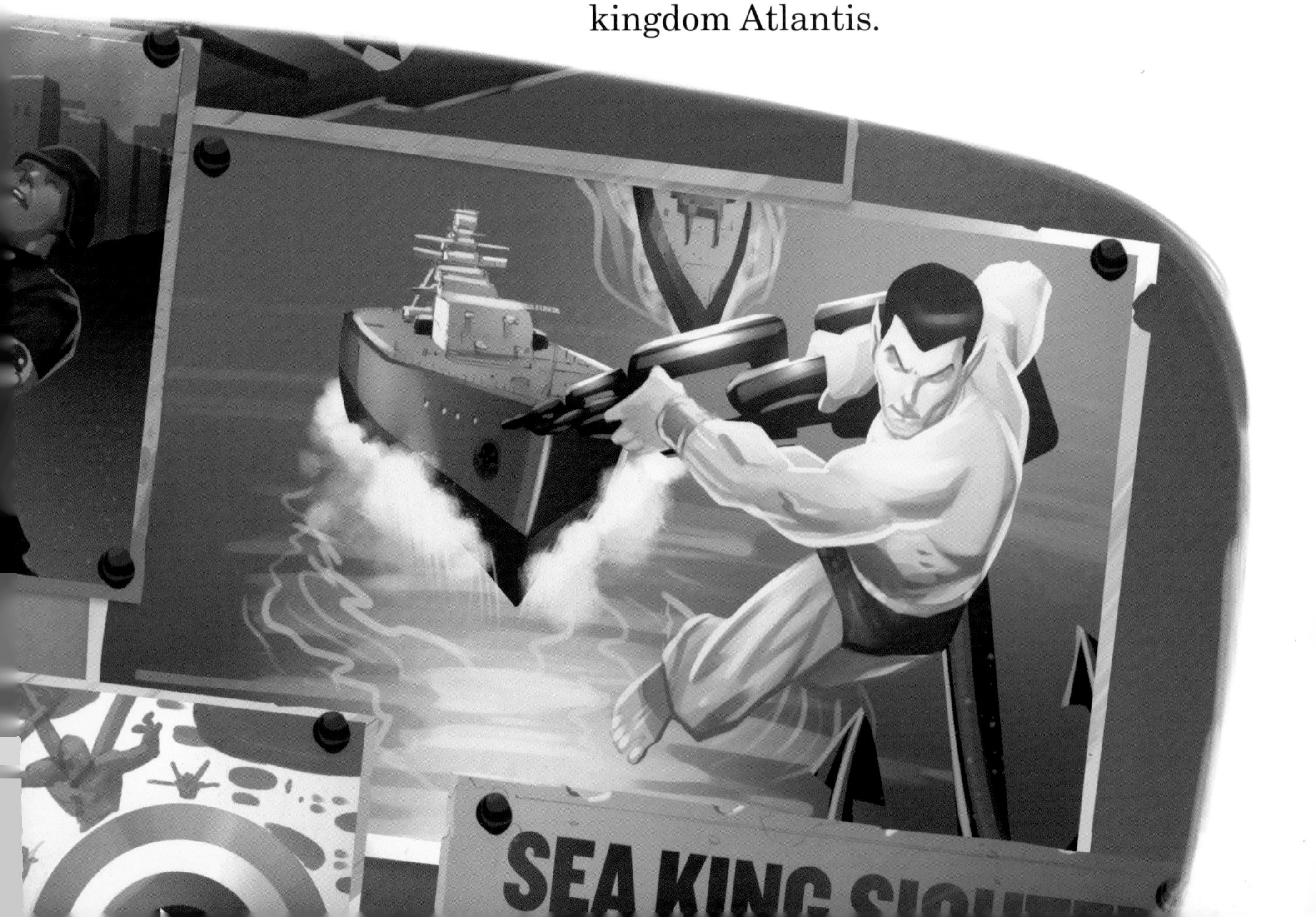
SEA KING

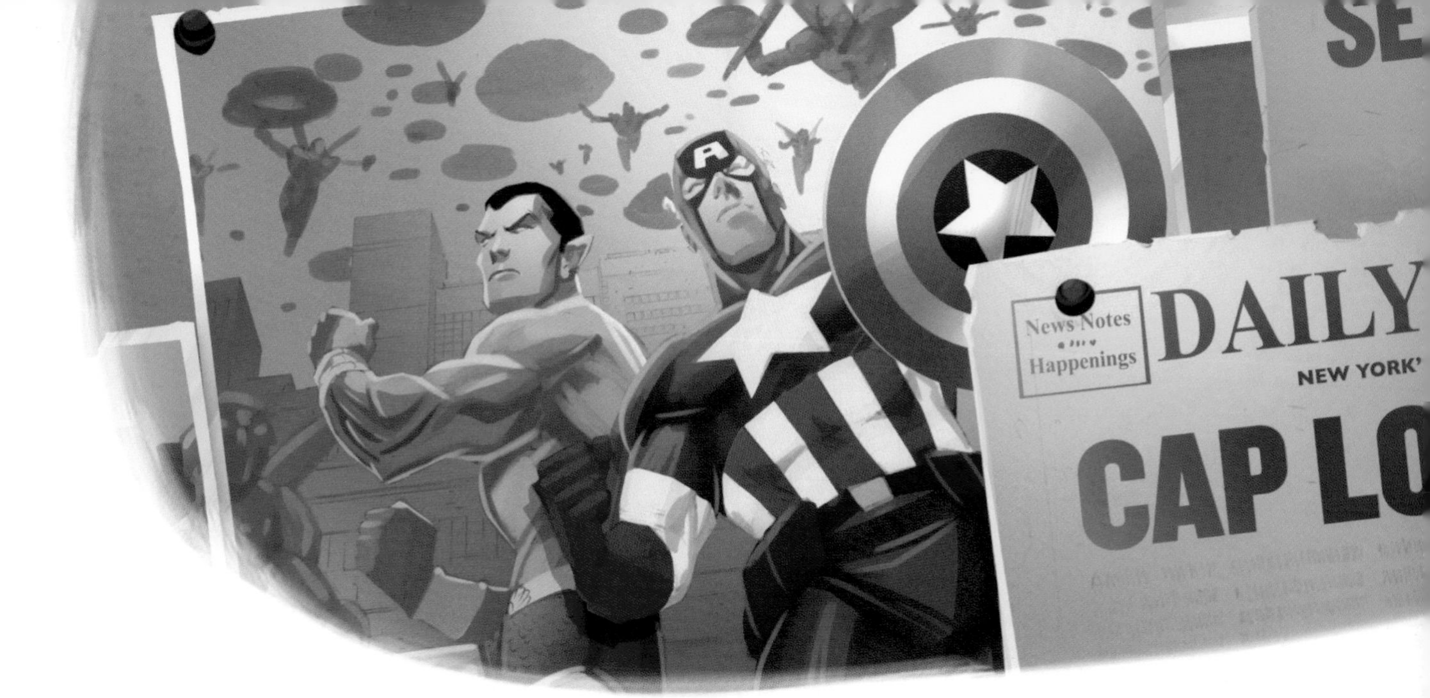
News Notes
Happenings
DAILY
NEW YORK'
CAP LO

Sometimes the two heroes fought together against enemy armies, evil madmen—even alien invasions.

But then, without warning, the heroes suddenly **disappeared.**

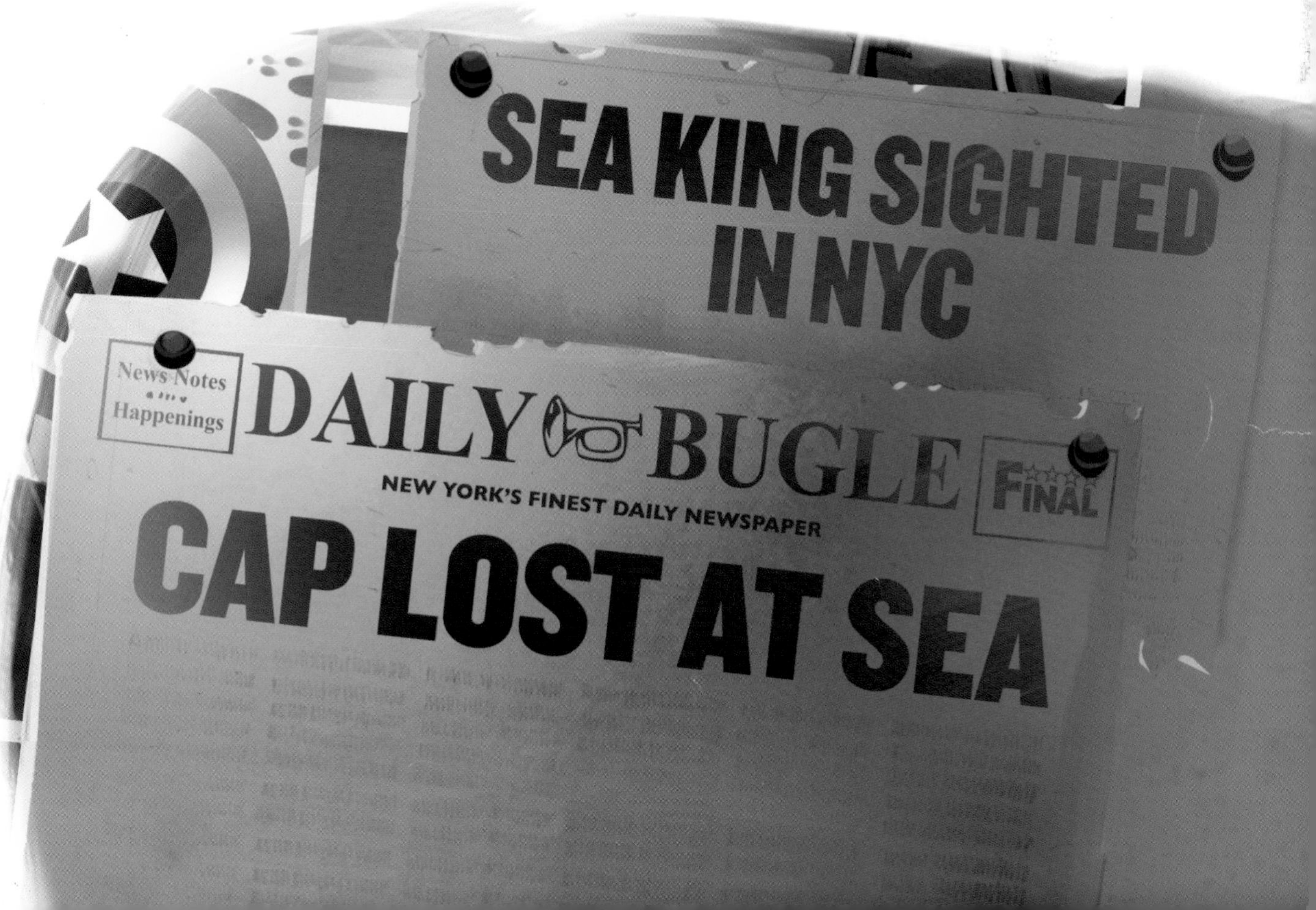
SEA KING SIGHTED IN NYC
News Notes
Happenings
DAILY BUGLE
FINAL
NEW YORK'S FINEST DAILY NEWSPAPER
CAP LOST AT SEA

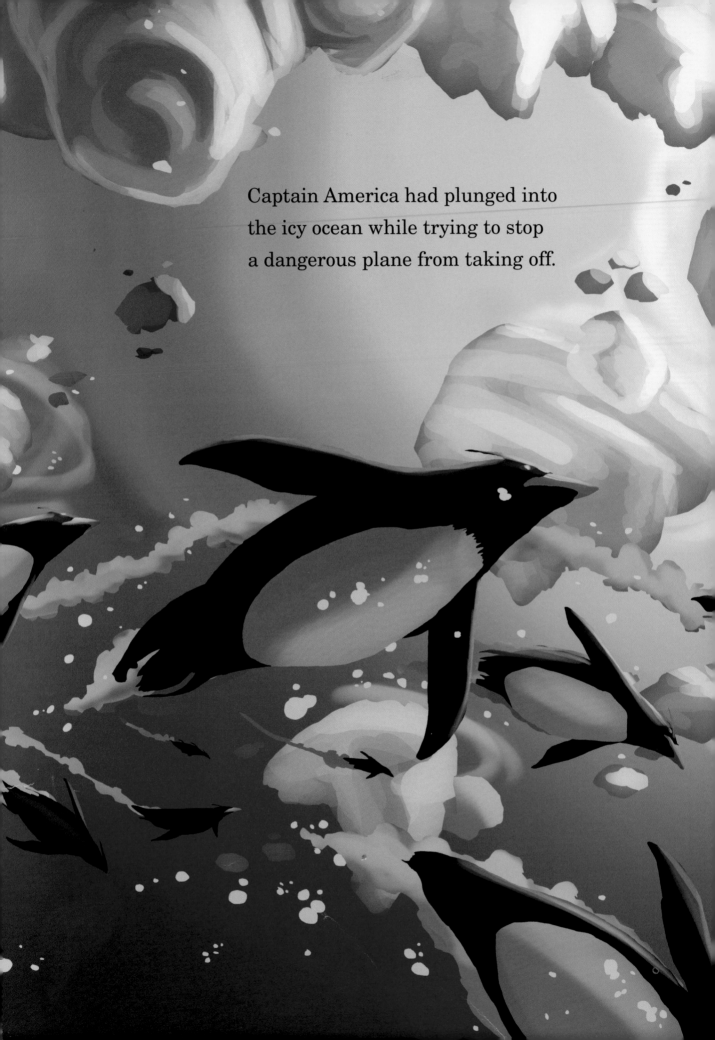

Captain America had plunged into
the icy ocean while trying to stop
a dangerous plane from taking off.

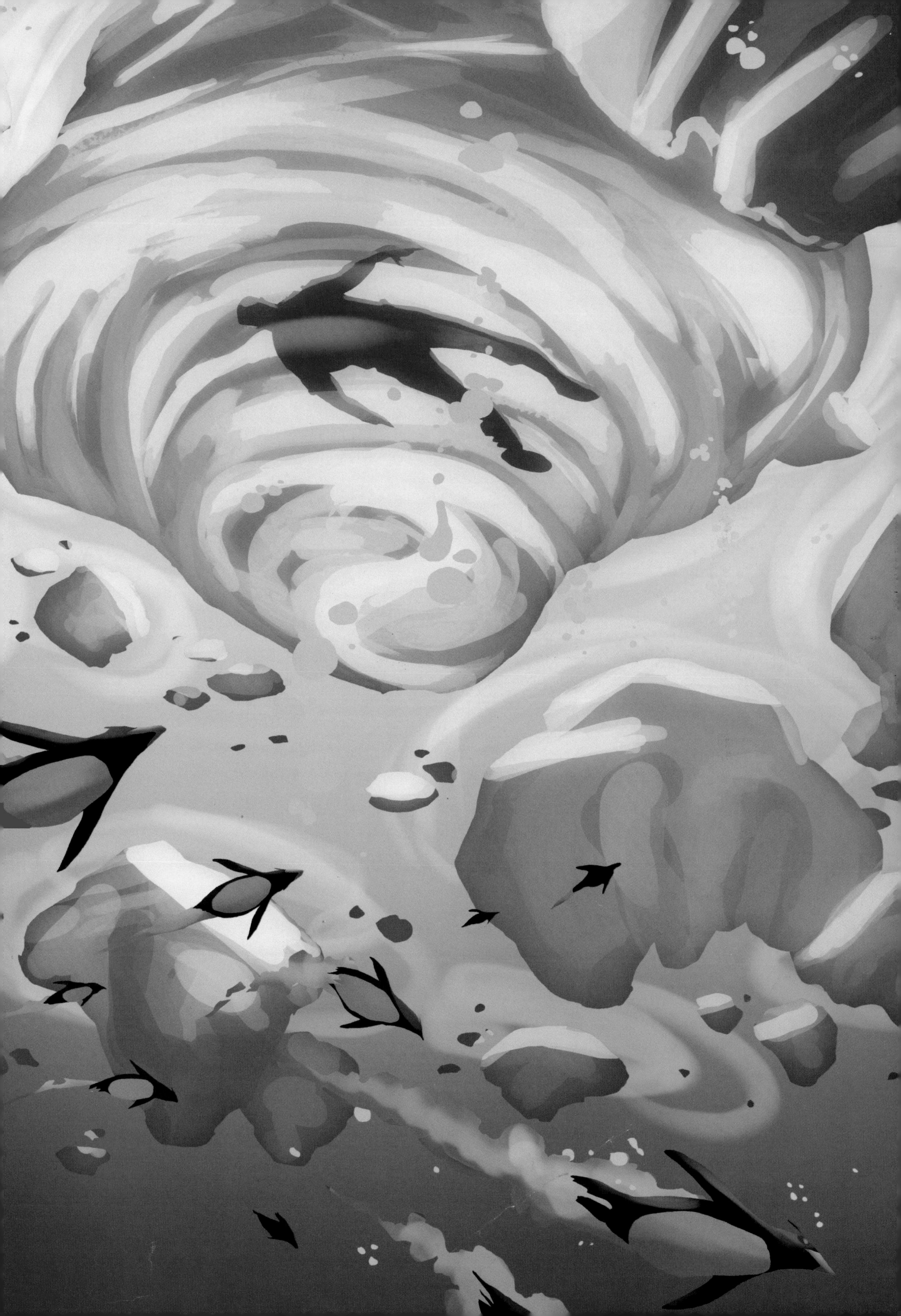

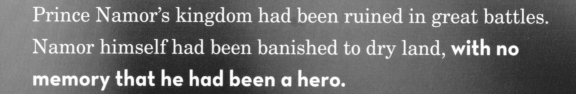

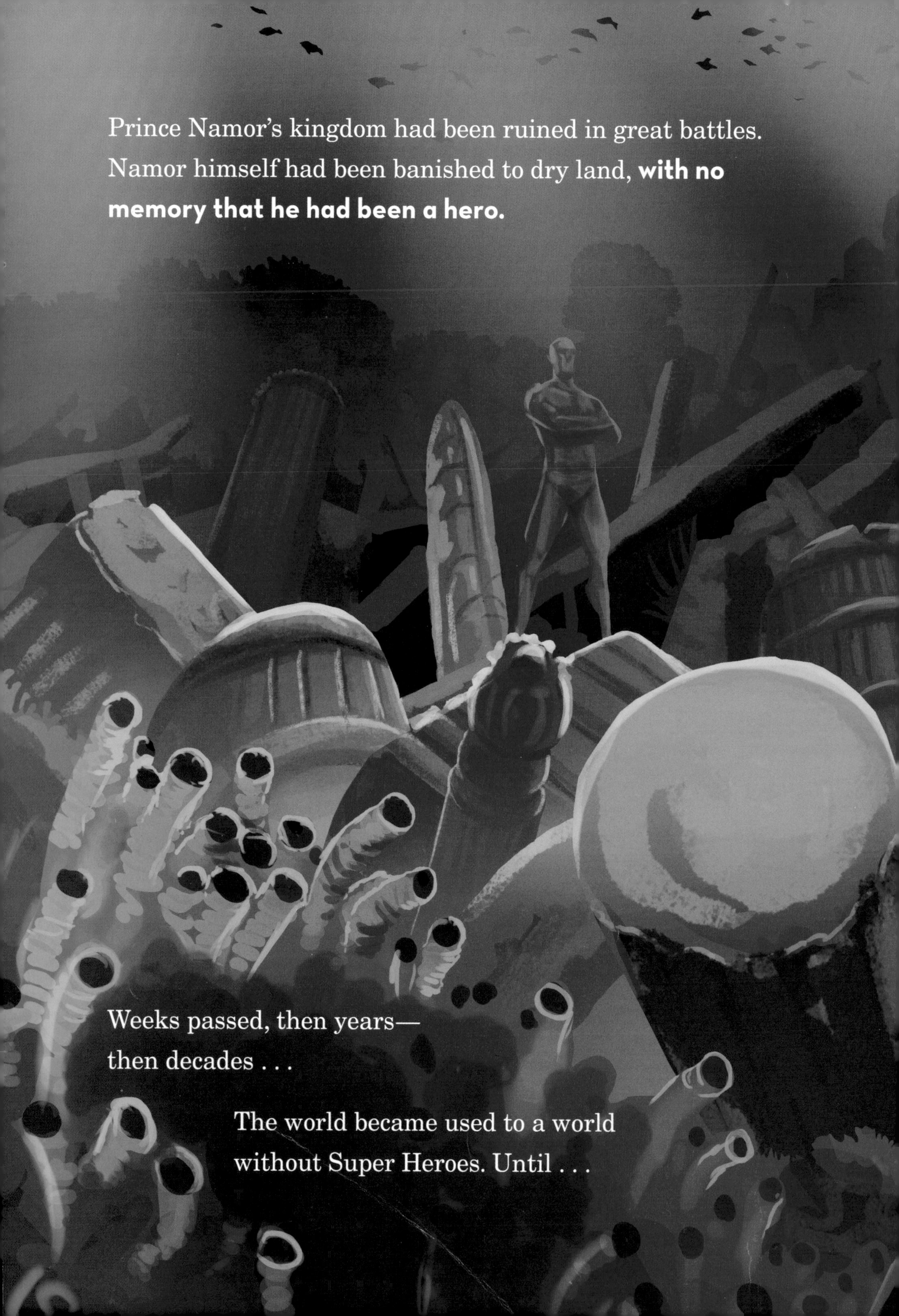

Prince Namor's kingdom had been ruined in great battles. Namor himself had been banished to dry land, **with no memory that he had been a hero.**

Weeks passed, then years—
then decades . . .

The world became used to a world
without Super Heroes. Until . . .

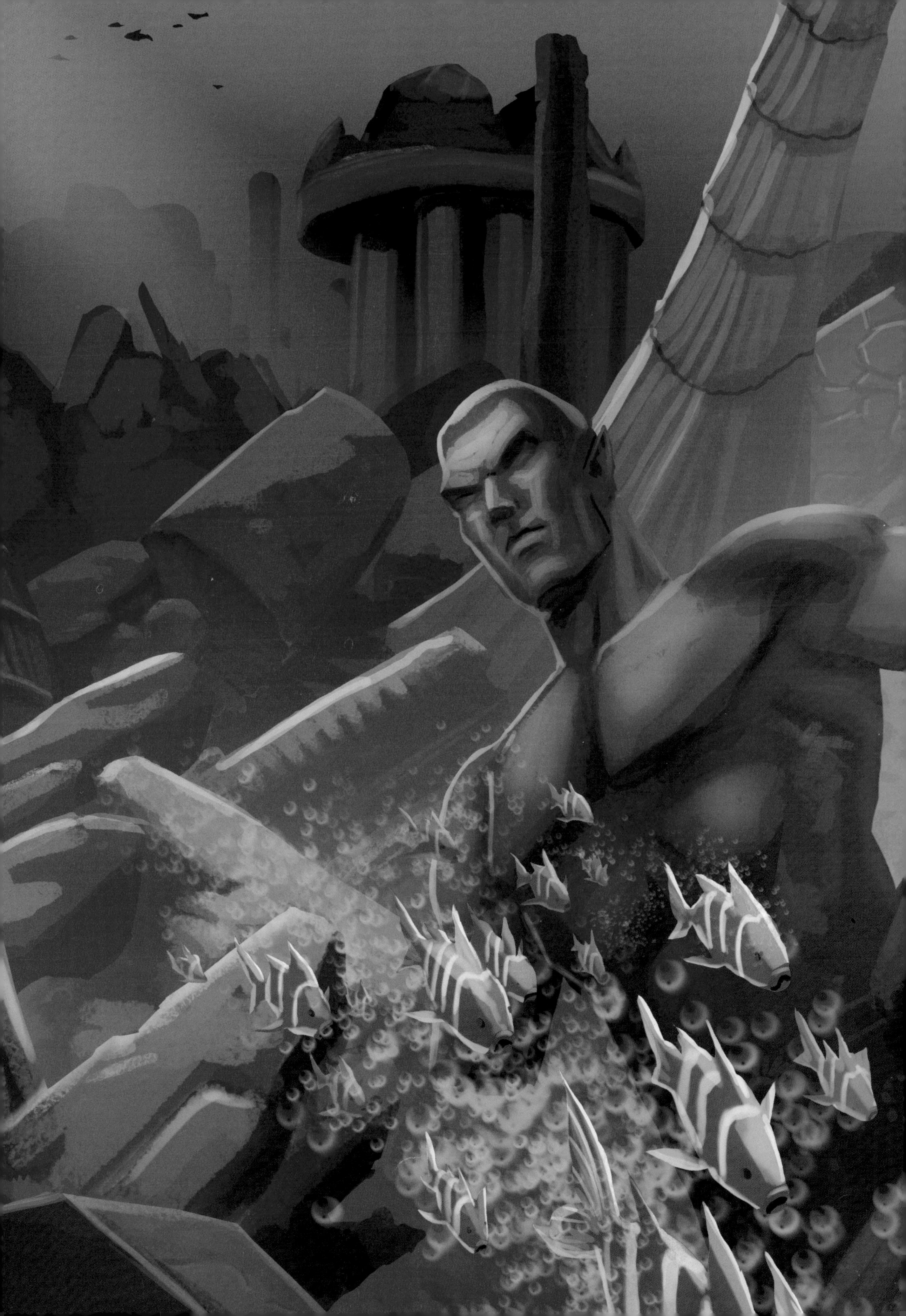

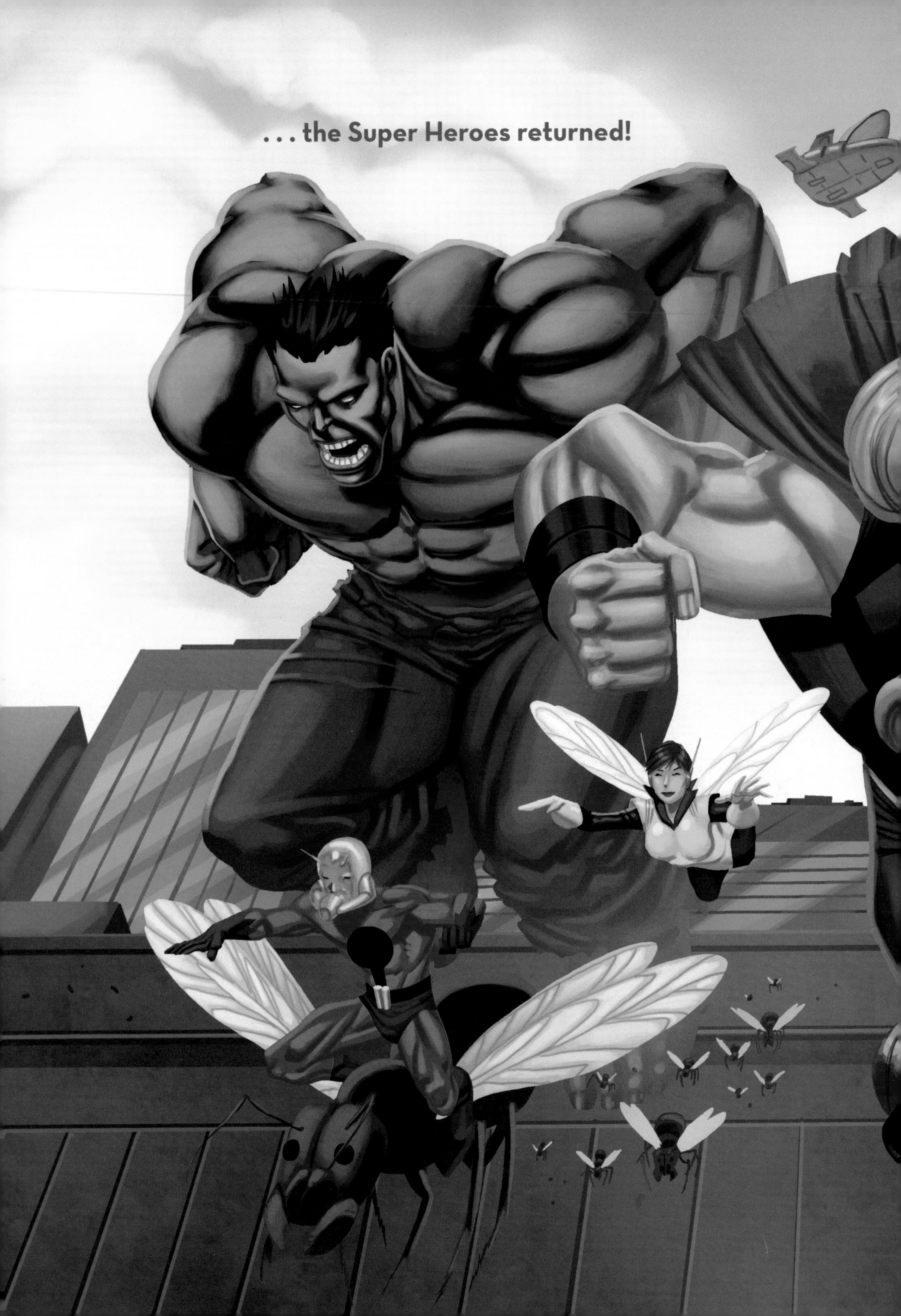
. . . the Super Heroes returned!

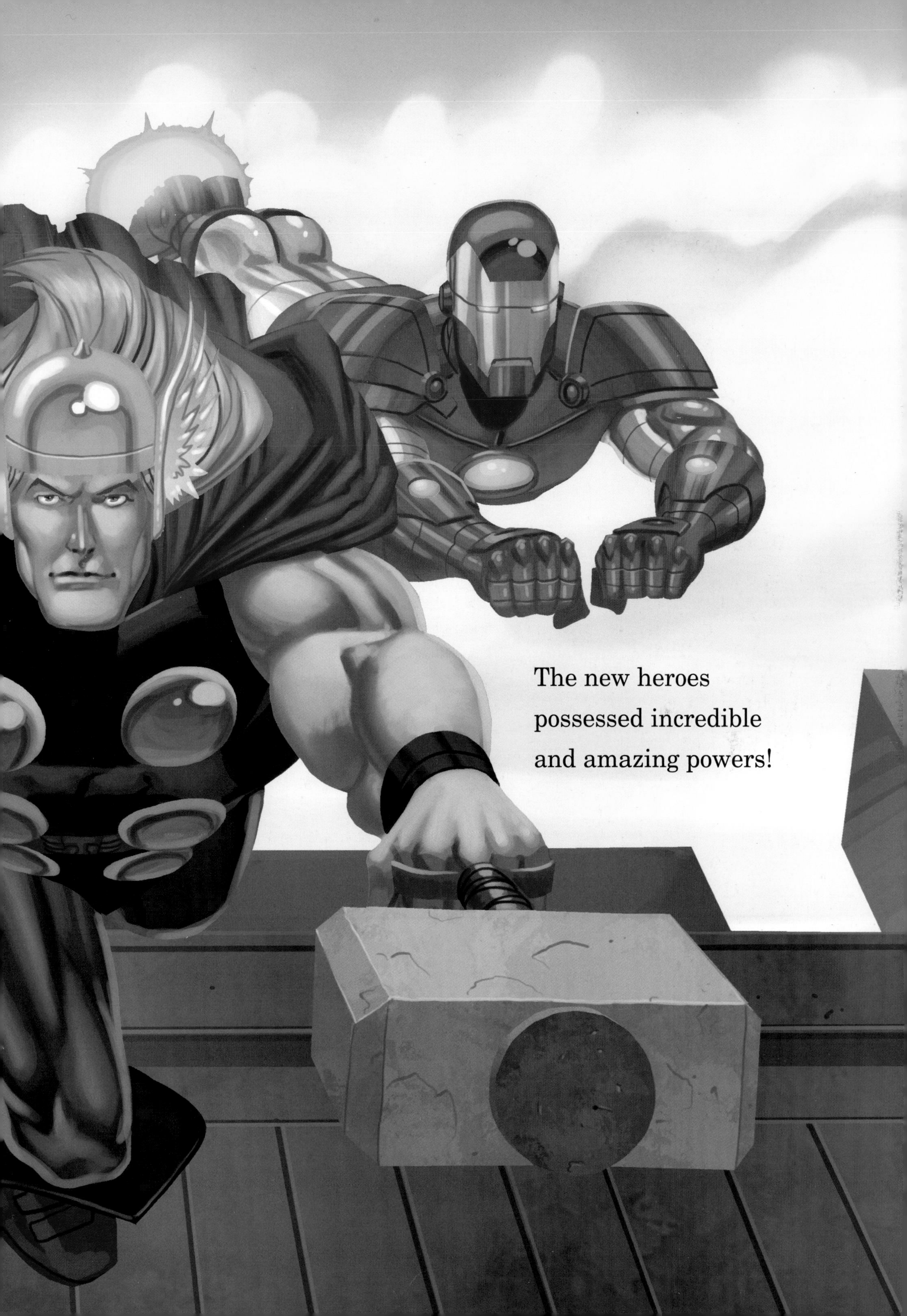

The new heroes
possessed incredible
and amazing powers!

Thor could summon all the might of thunder.

TONY STARK wore powerful armor to become **Iron Man.**

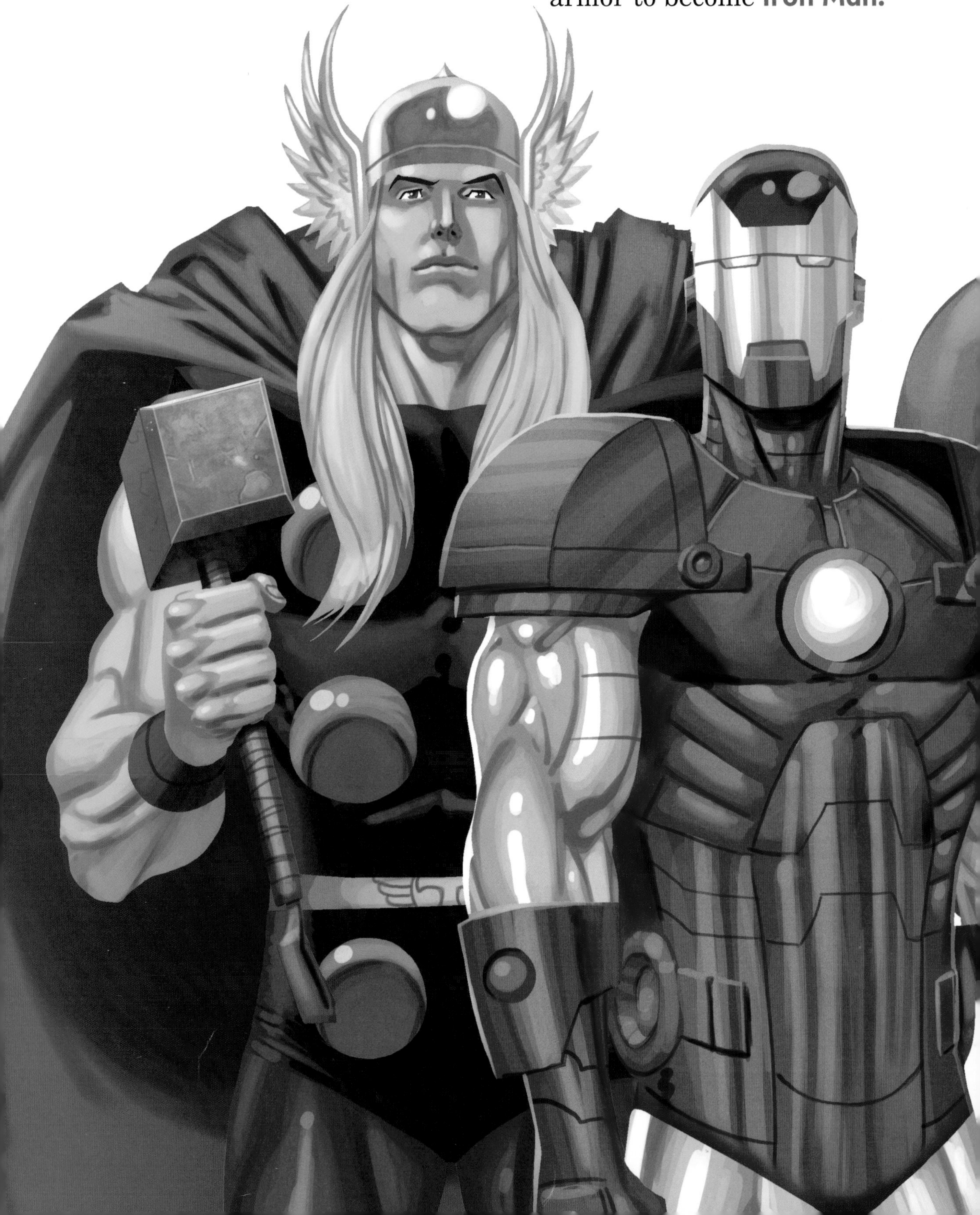

Ant-Man and **Wasp** could become bigger or smaller.

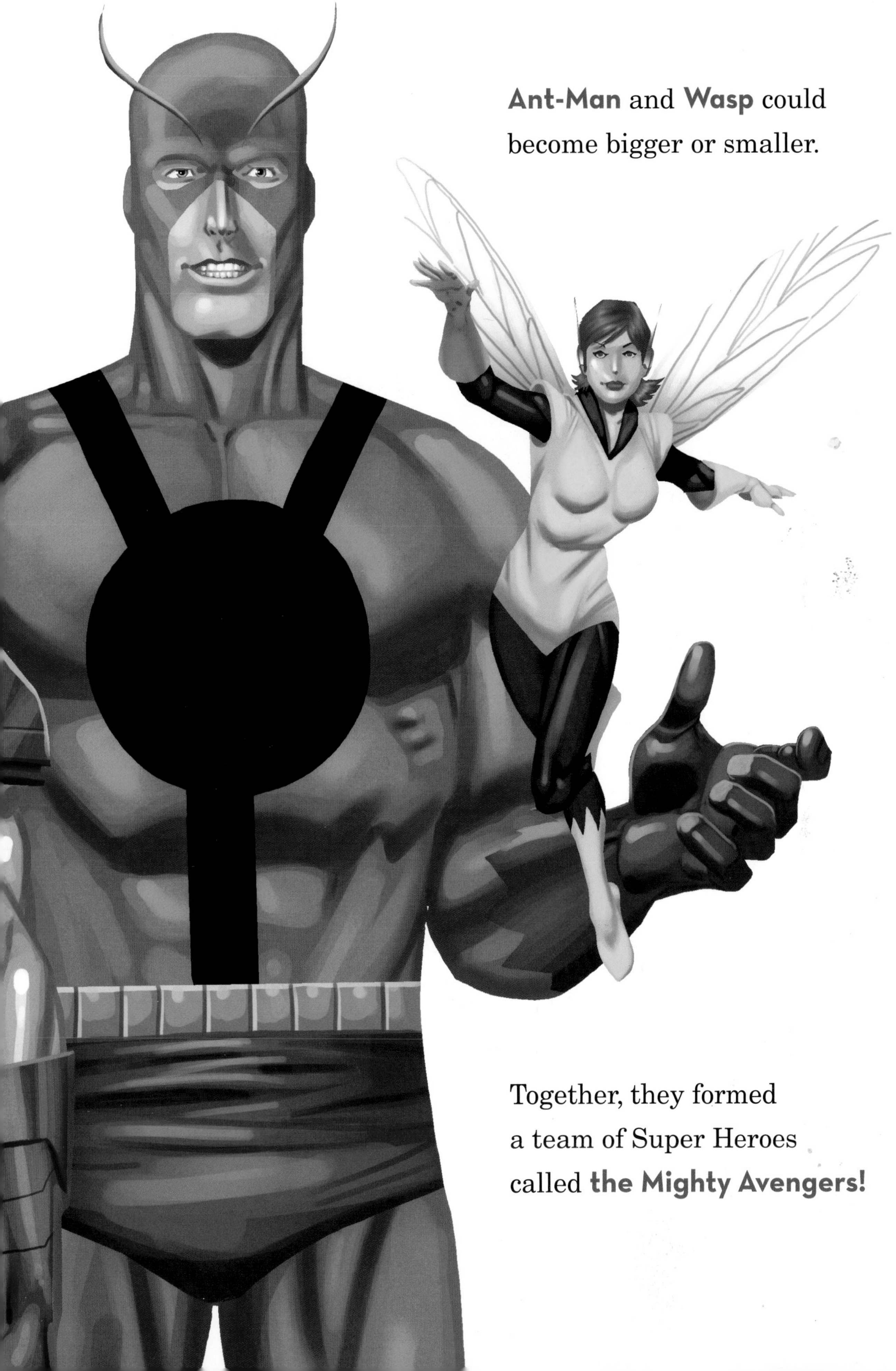

Together, they formed a team of Super Heroes called **the Mighty Avengers!**

The Avengers had come to this spot in search of their friend **the Incredible Hulk**, who had gone missing after the team's last battle.

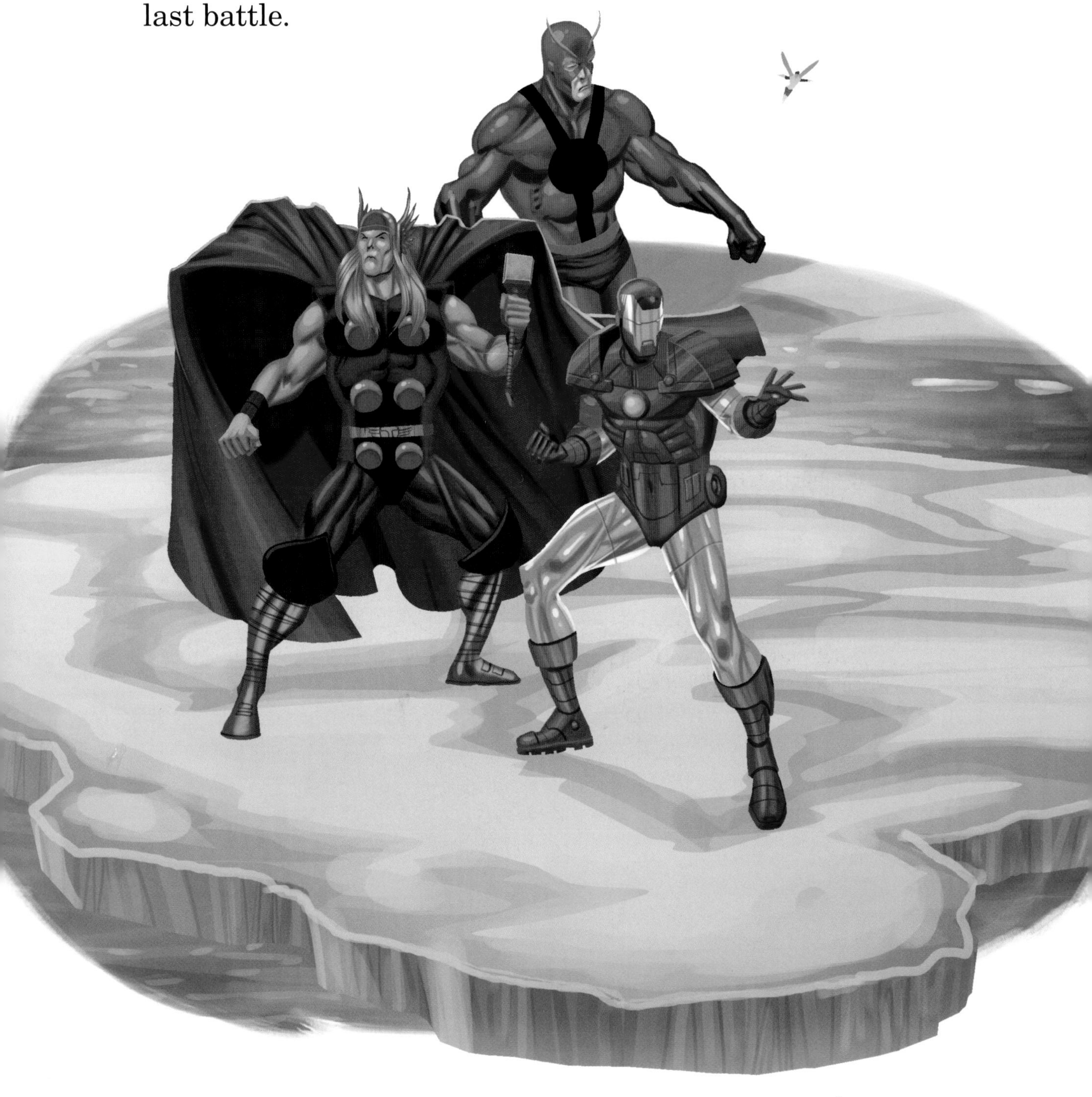

They also wanted to investigate a rumor they had heard—that after all these long years, **Namor had returned.**

But none of them were prepared for what they saw next. . . .

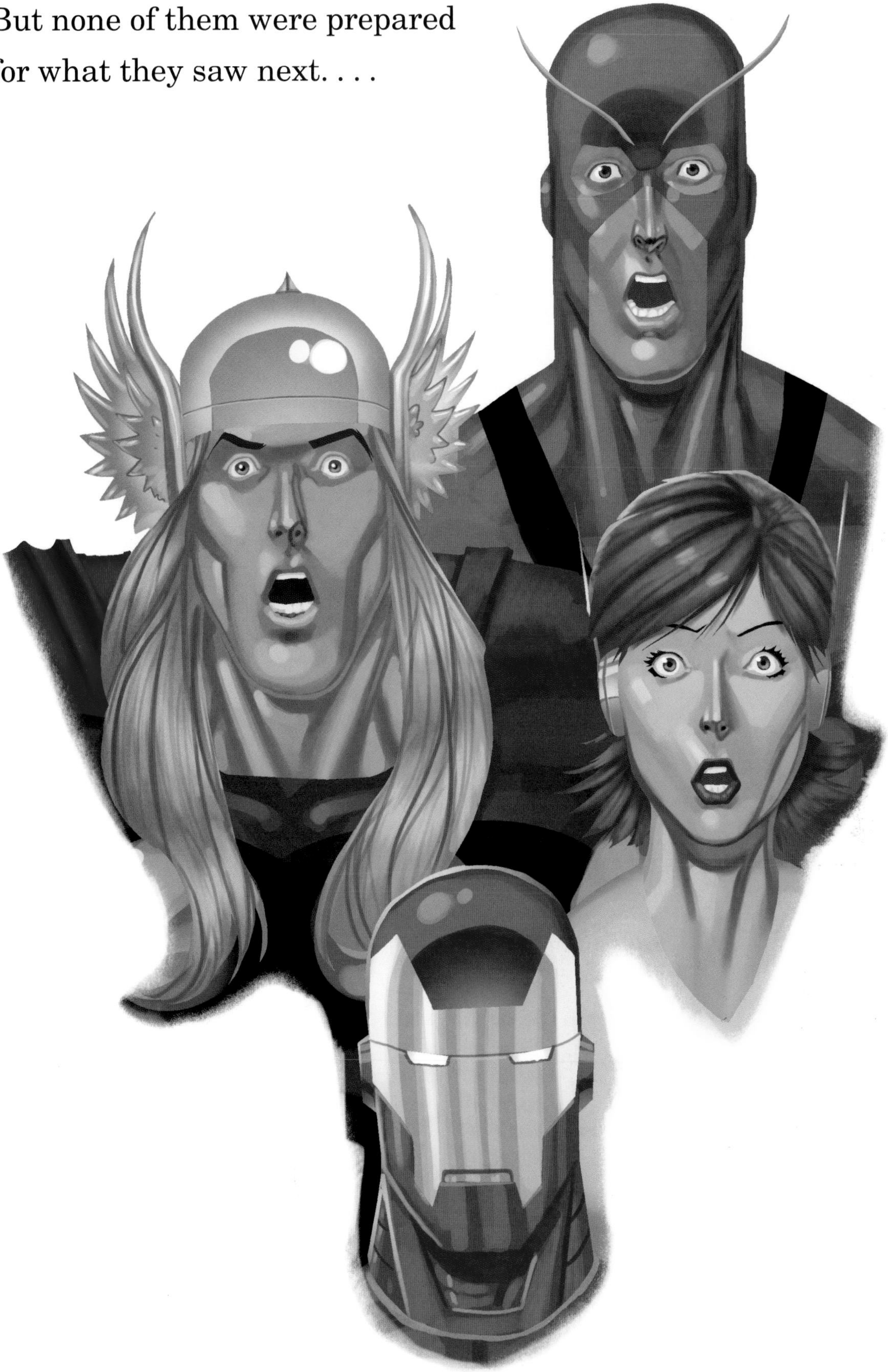

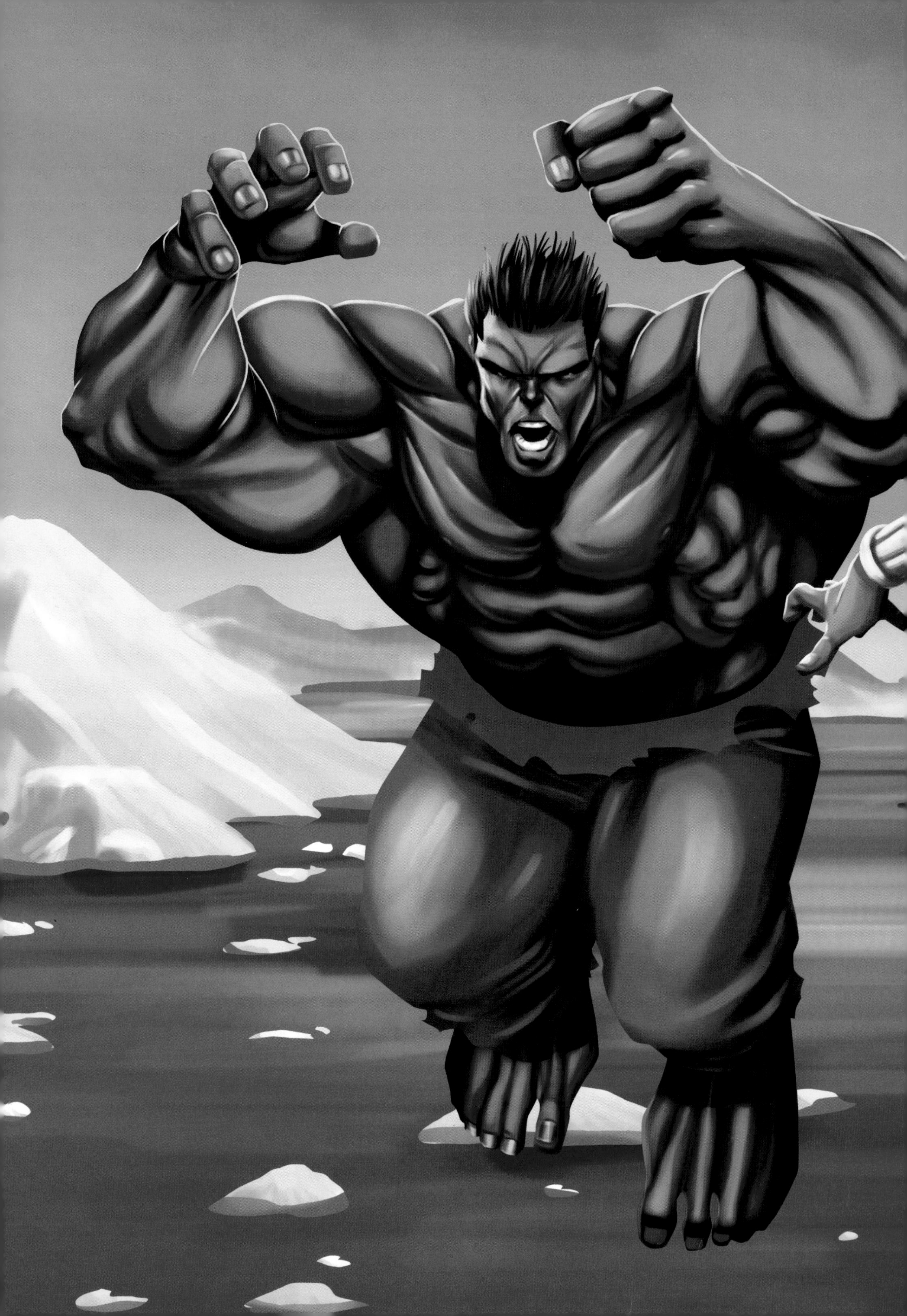

The Hulk was with Namor, who had indeed returned. But the Atlantean seemed **very angry**—not at all like the hero they had heard tales of.

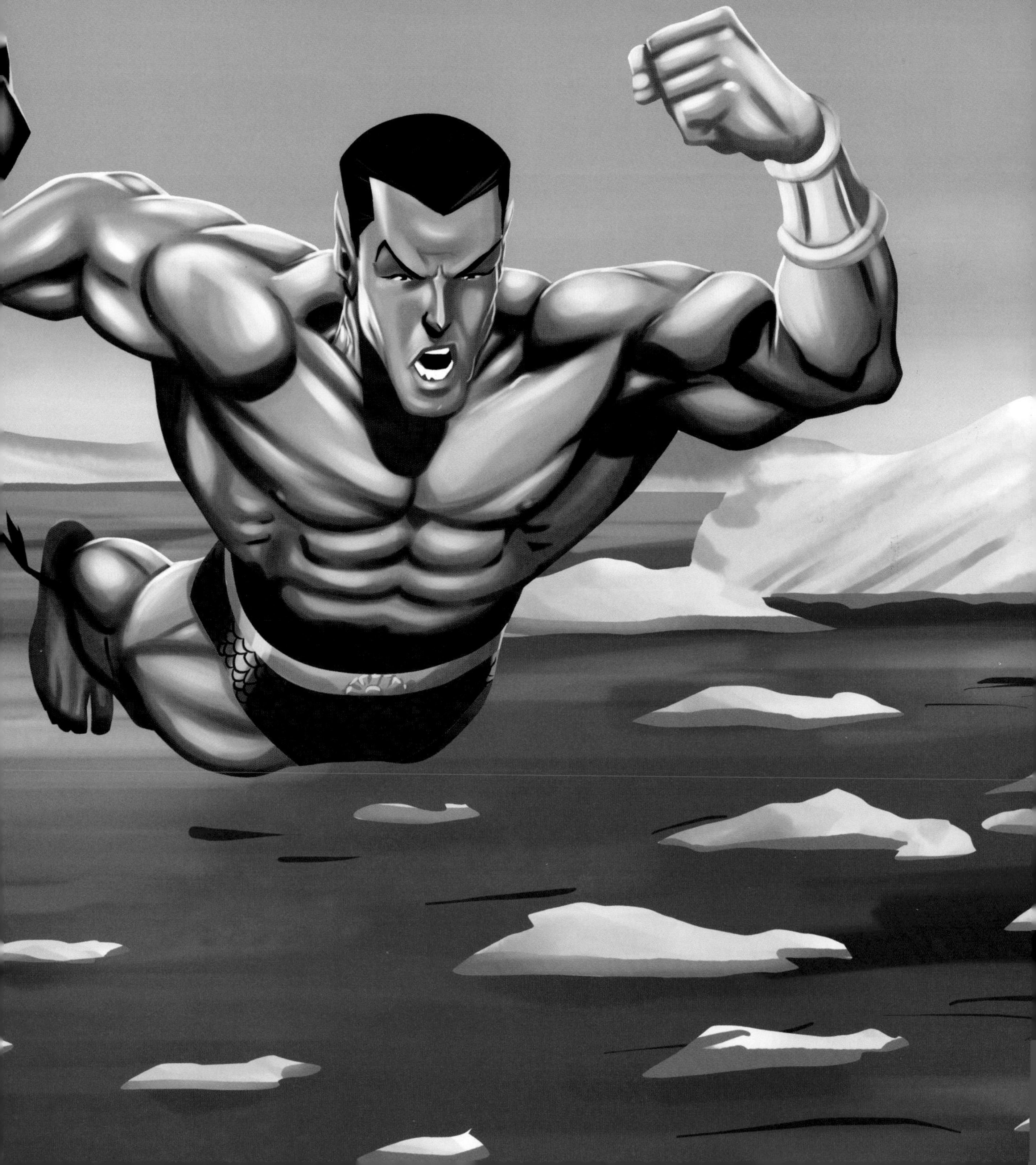

The heroes knew that **Namor's powers came from the water**, and in a place like this, with lots of it nearby, he would be hard to beat.

Having the Hulk on his side made it even harder.

Namor told the Avengers that his kingdom, **Atlantis**, was in ruins. He thought humans had destroyed it. To get revenge, he planned to defeat Earth's Mightiest Heroes—**the Avengers!** Then he would rule over the human race!

The Avengers couldn't figure out why the Hulk was fighting alongside him.

The Hulk was strong and tough to beat.

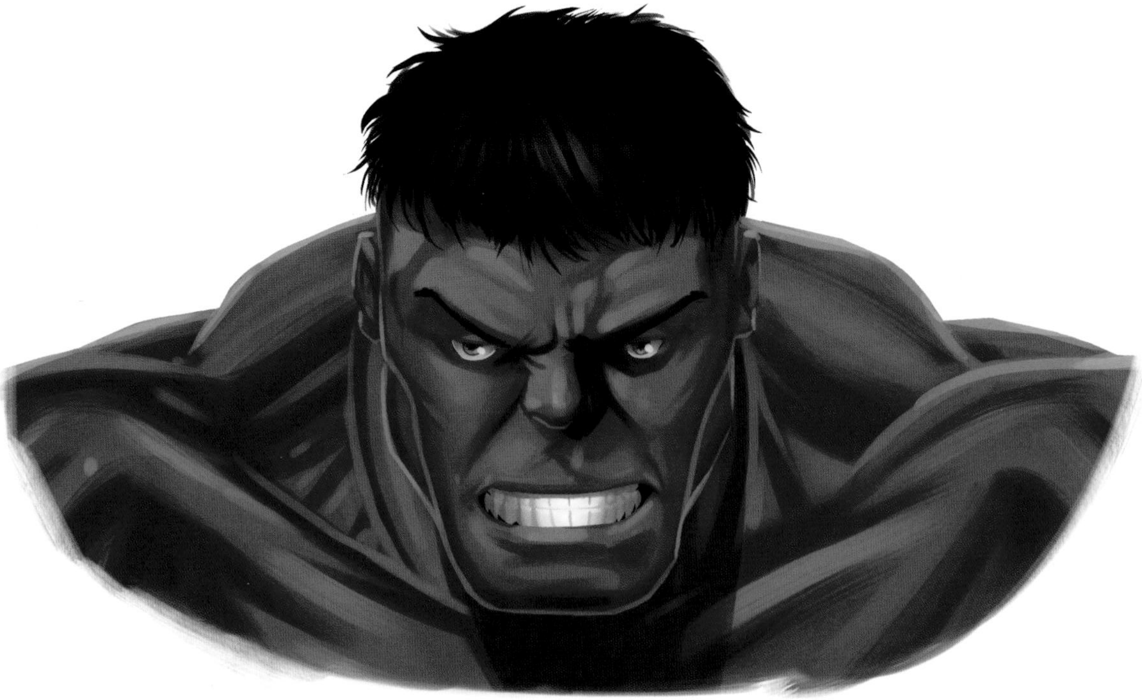

But he was their friend.

He was a hero.

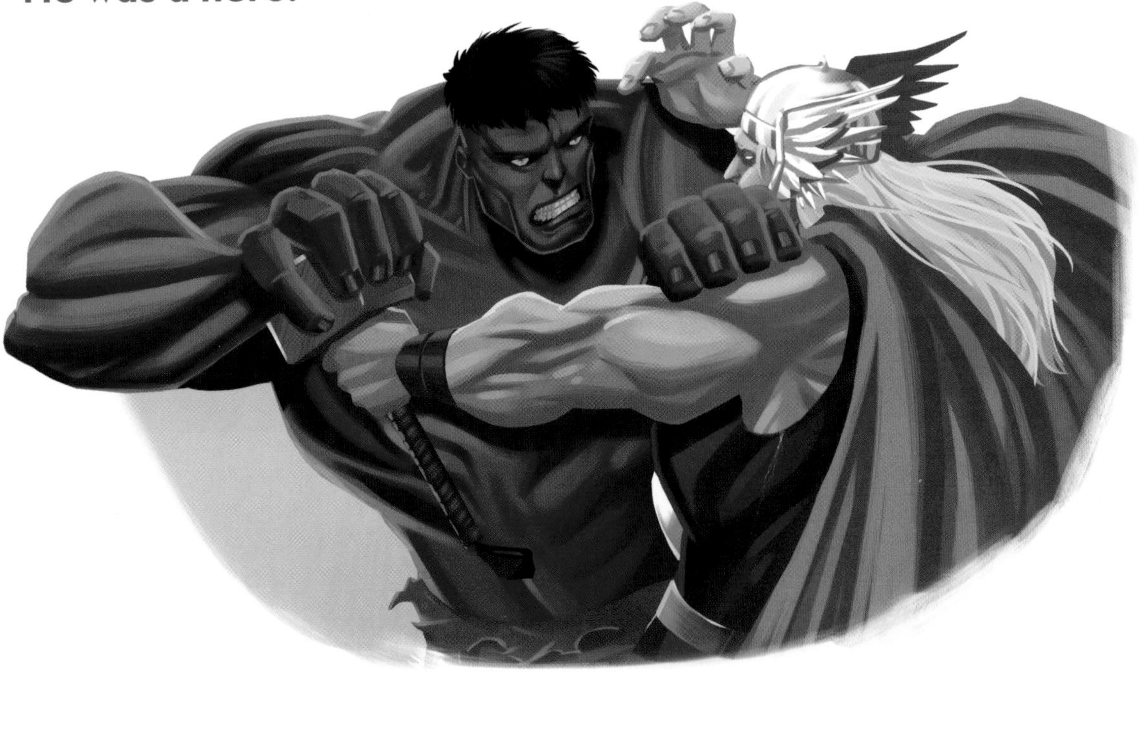

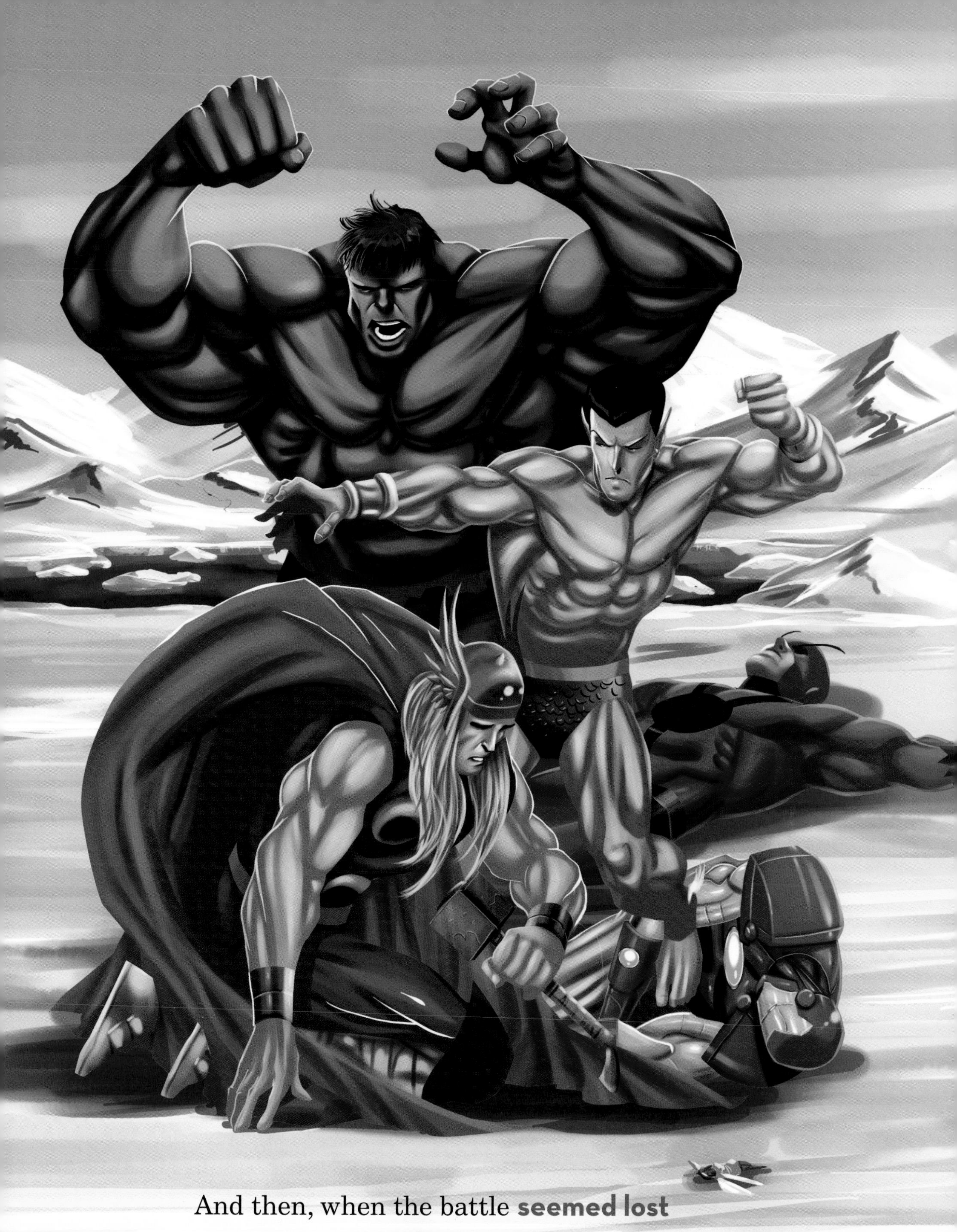

And then, when the battle **seemed lost**
and the last Avenger was about to fall—

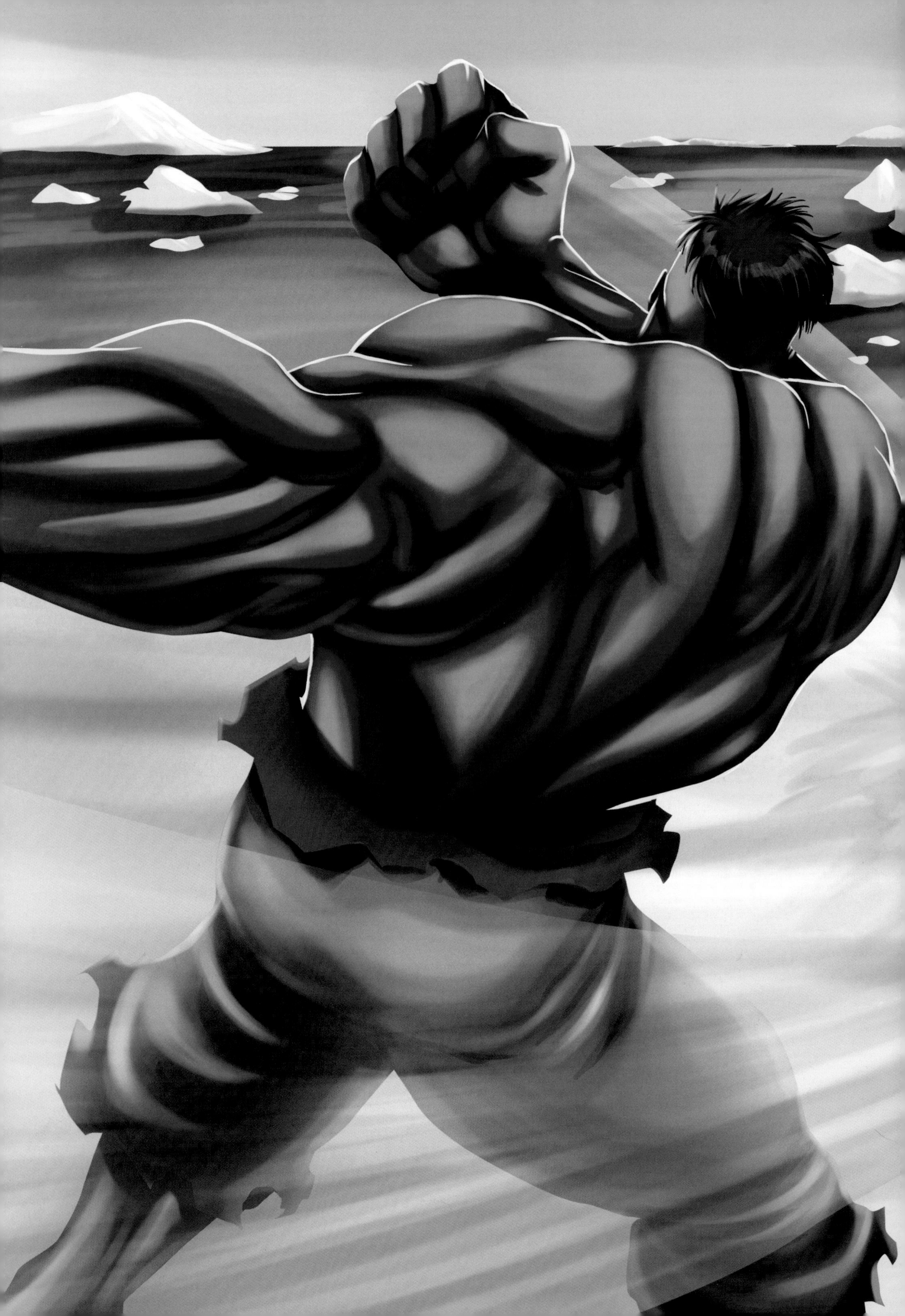

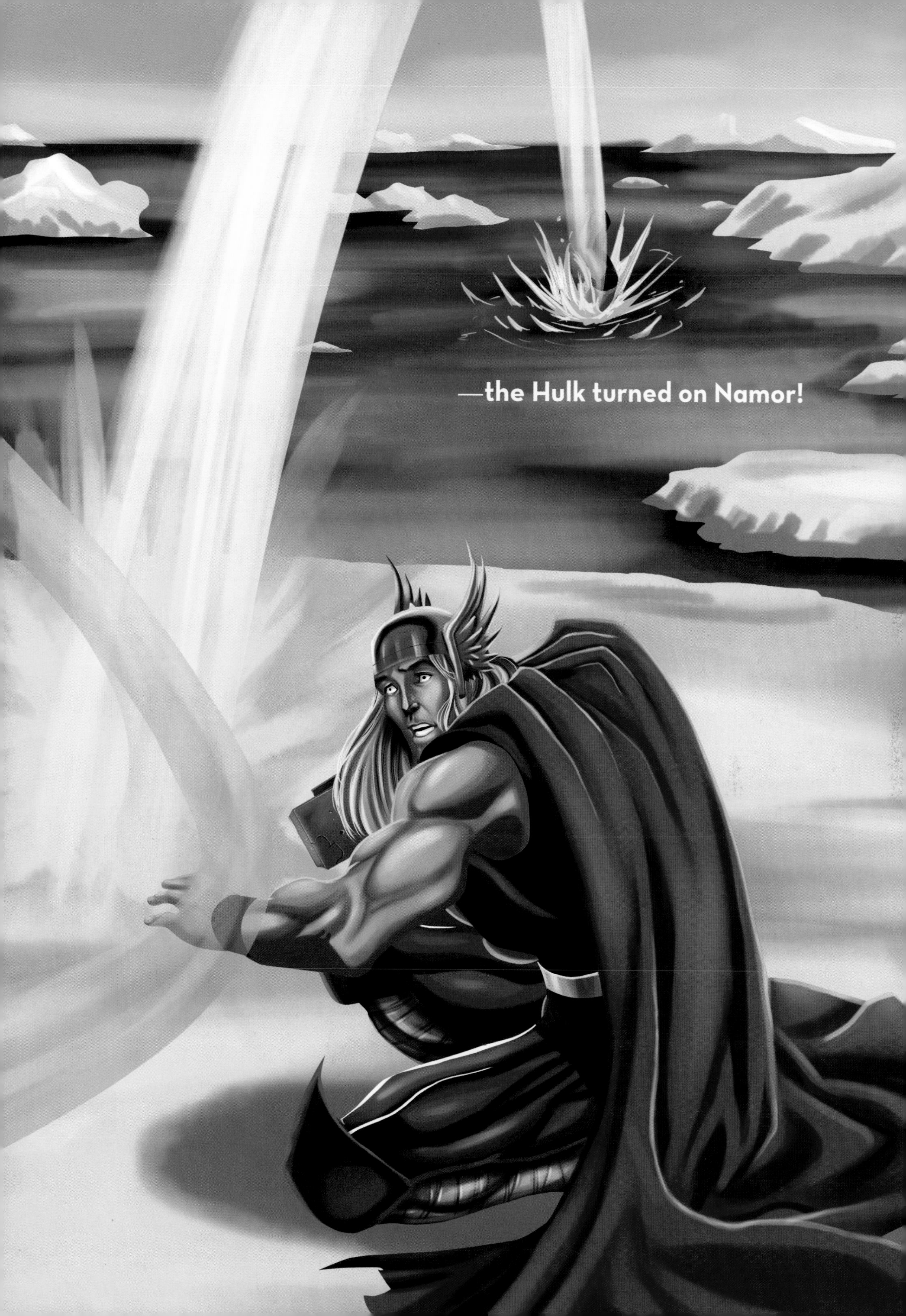

—the Hulk turned on Namor!

It had all been part of the Hulk's plan: he would make Namor think he was on his side, but in the end help the Avengers win the battle.

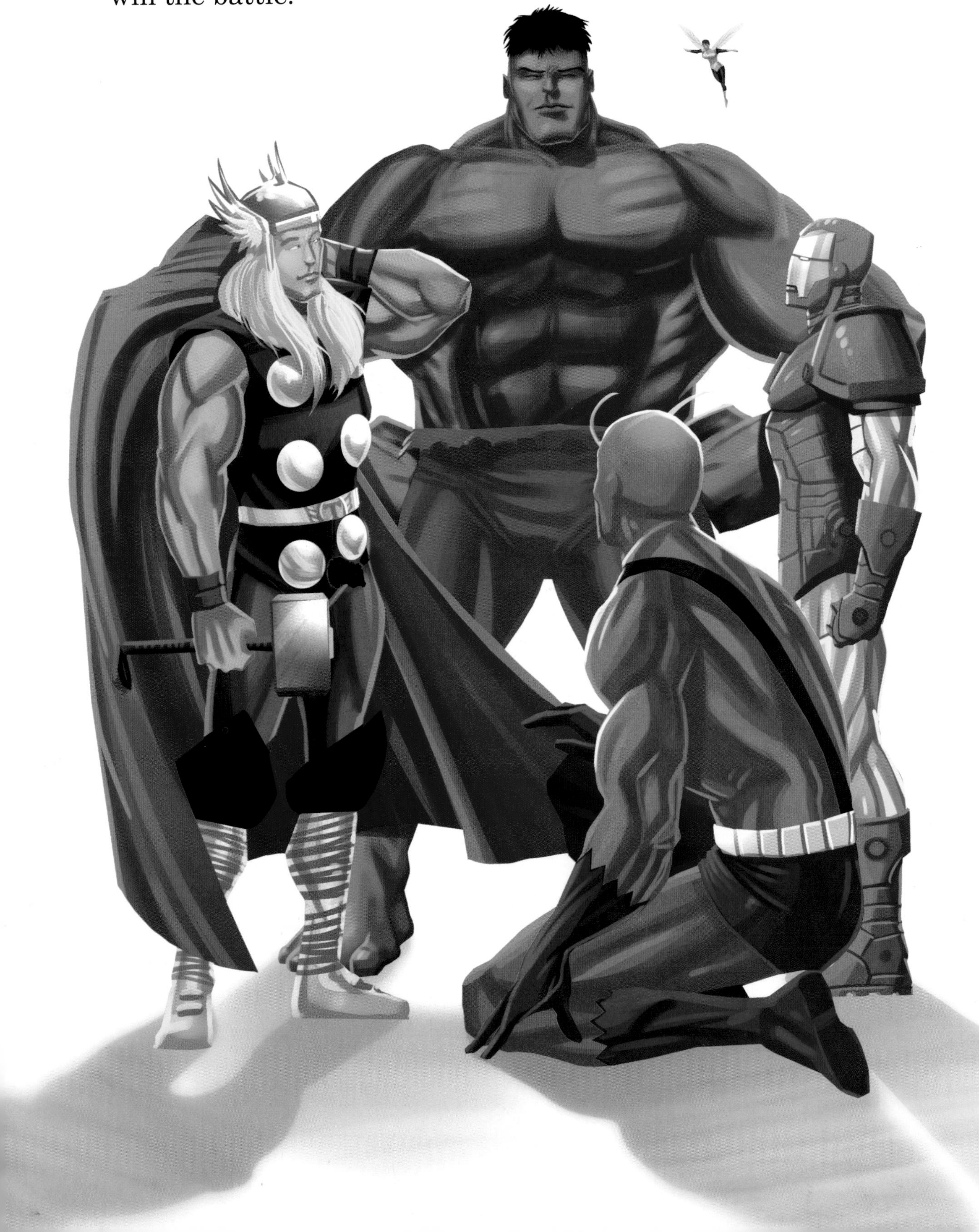

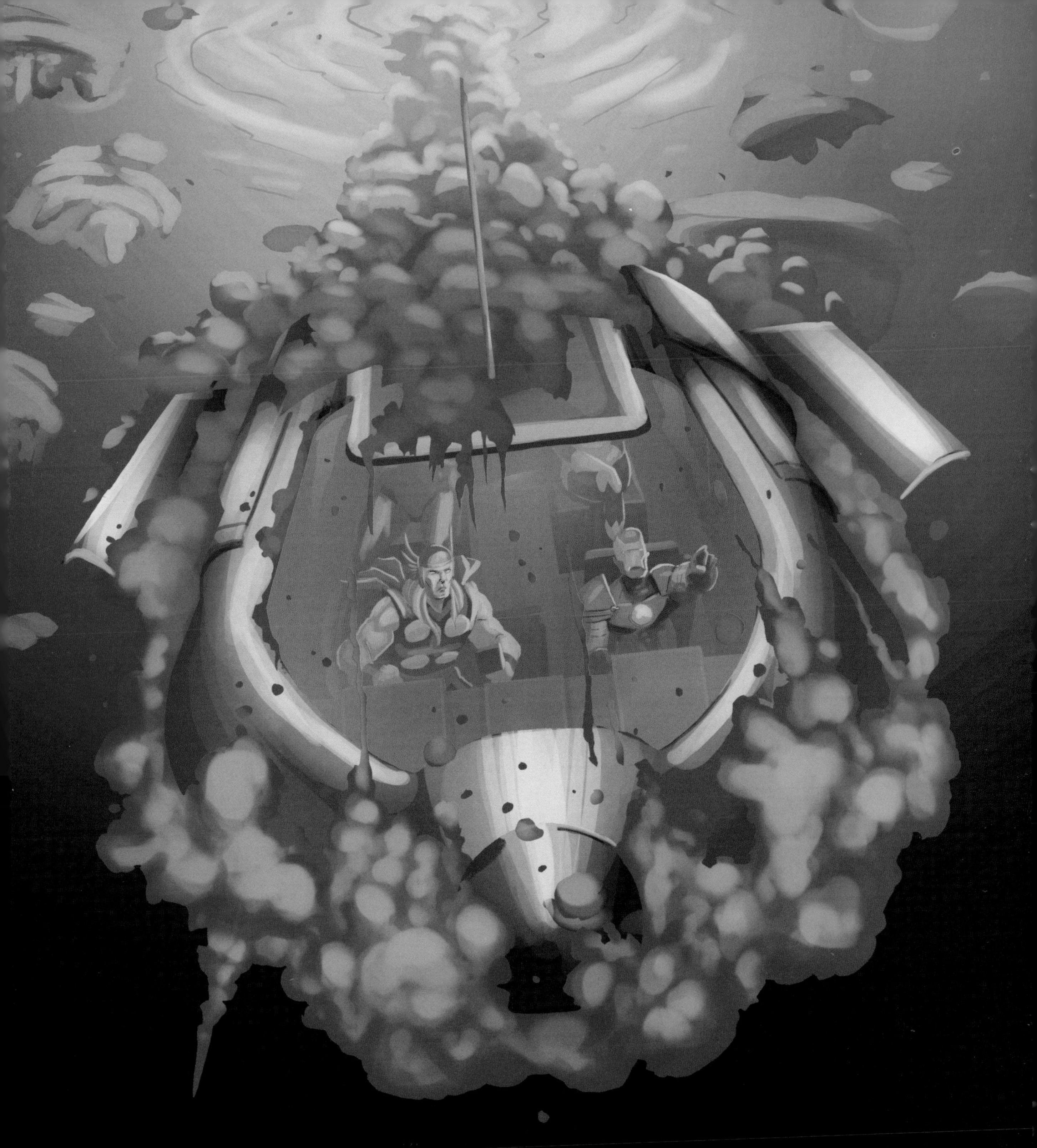

The Avengers couldn't let Namor escape. They jumped in their Quinjet and rushed into the water to go after the Sub-Mariner. But as soon as they were beneath the surface, **Iron Man noticed something. . . .**

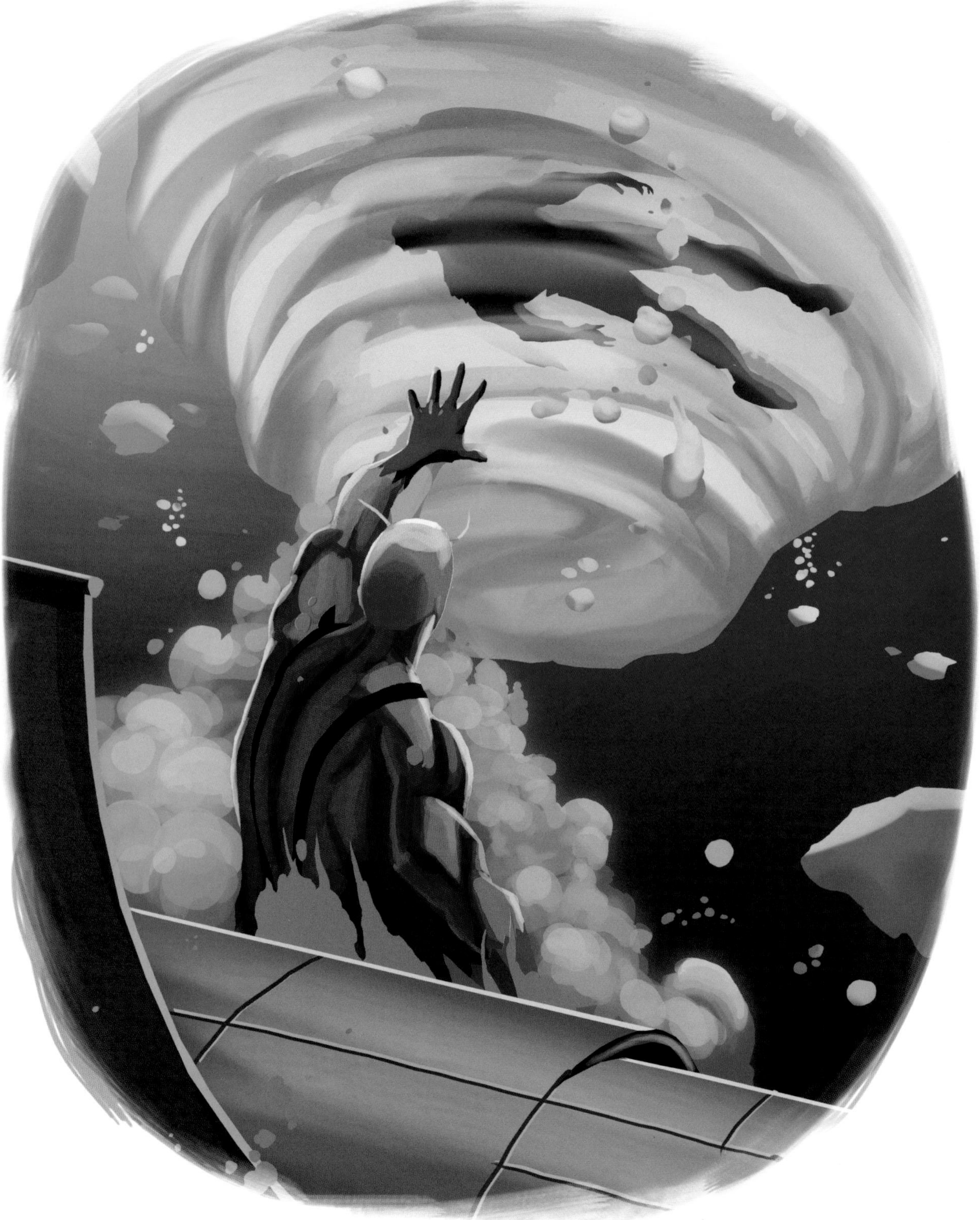

It was a man frozen in a block of ice.

Ant-Man swam out of the craft and grabbed him.

Ant-Man brought the frozen figure back to the Quinjet and placed him in the sick bay. Iron Man carefully warmed the ice with his repulsor rays to free the man.

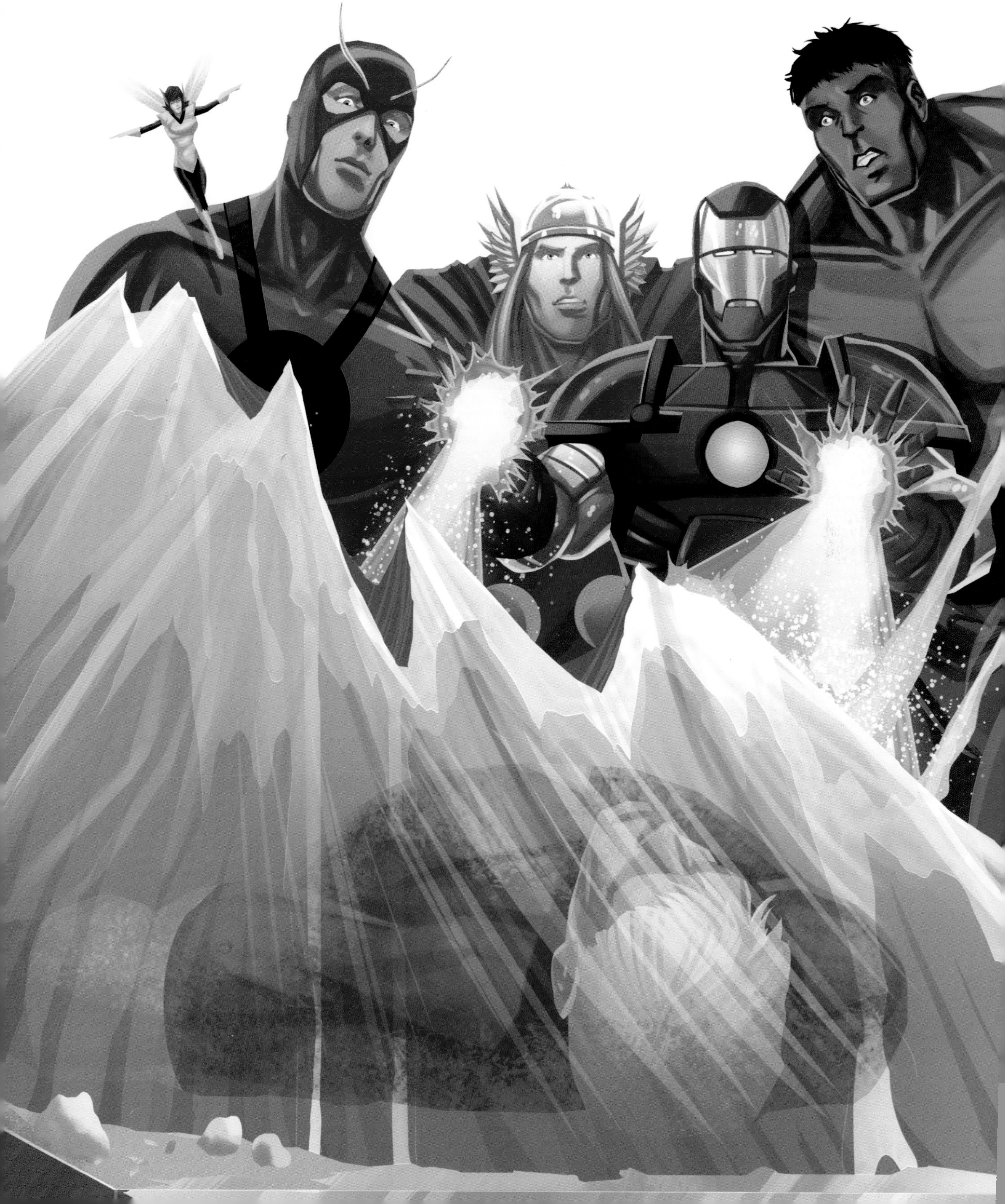

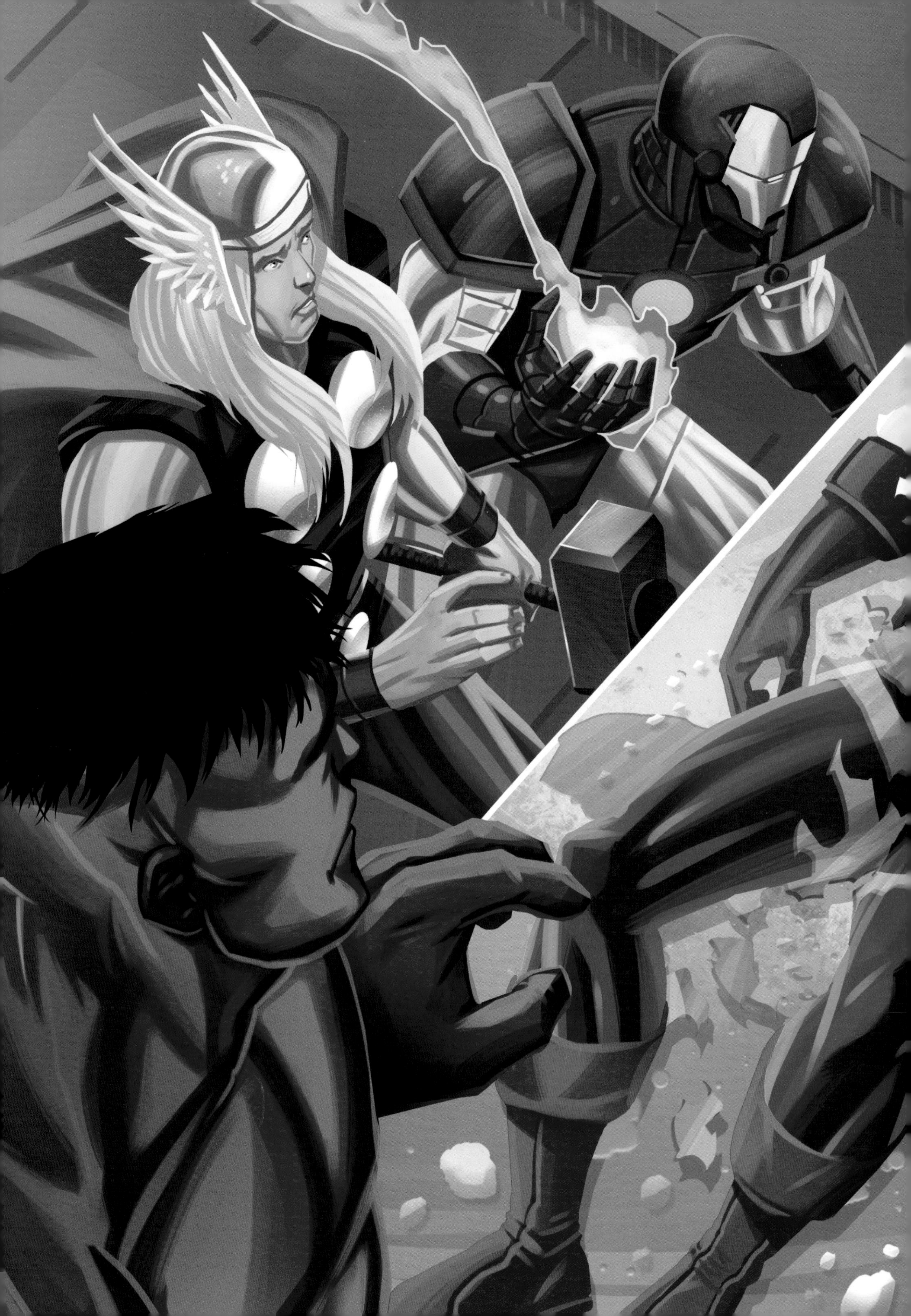

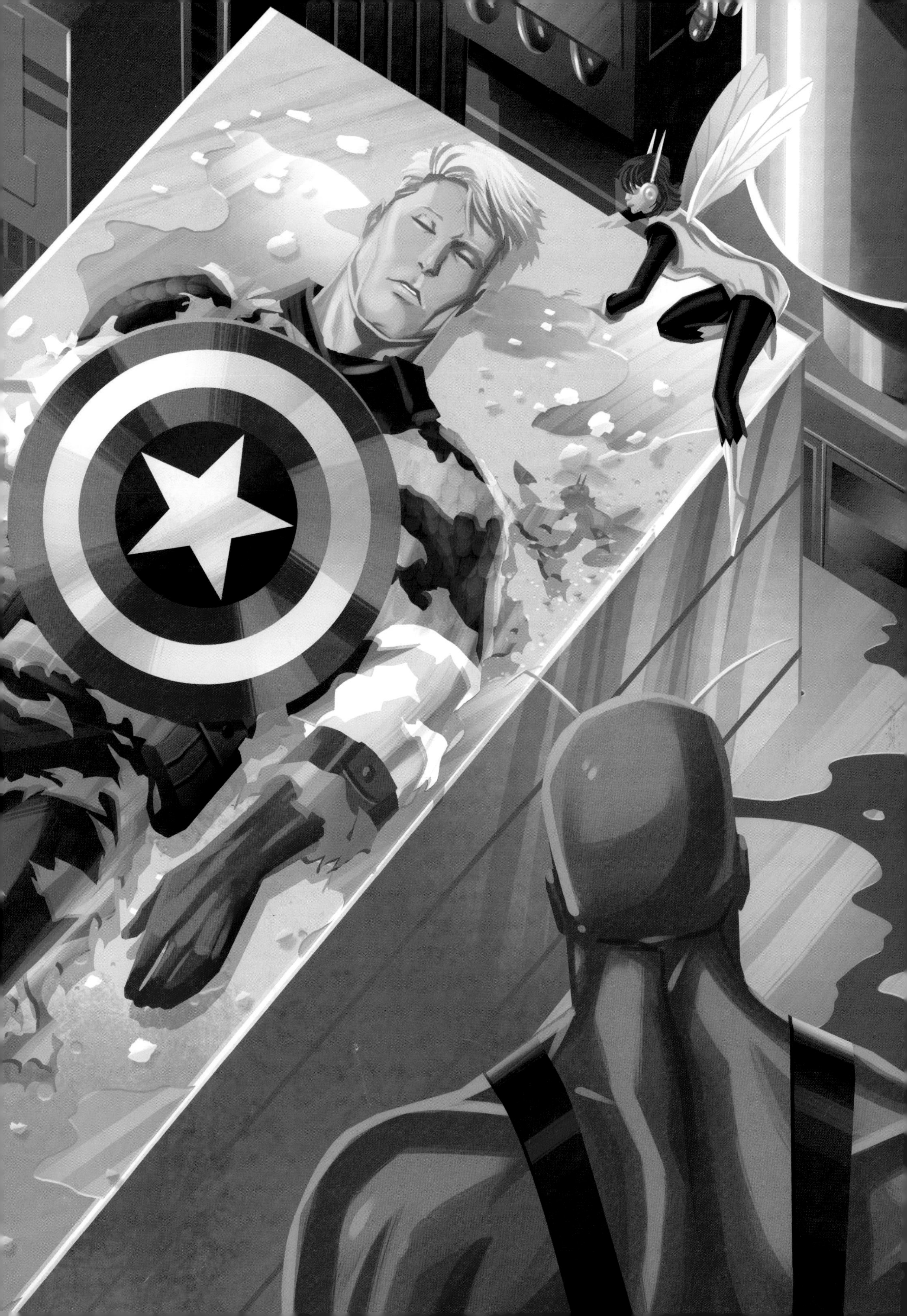

The Avengers couldn't believe what they were seeing.
They knew this man from history books.
He was Captain America!

Everything the Avengers did seemed to bother Captain America.
After all, he had no idea they were friendly. But Iron Man made
it clear when he handed him his shield . . .

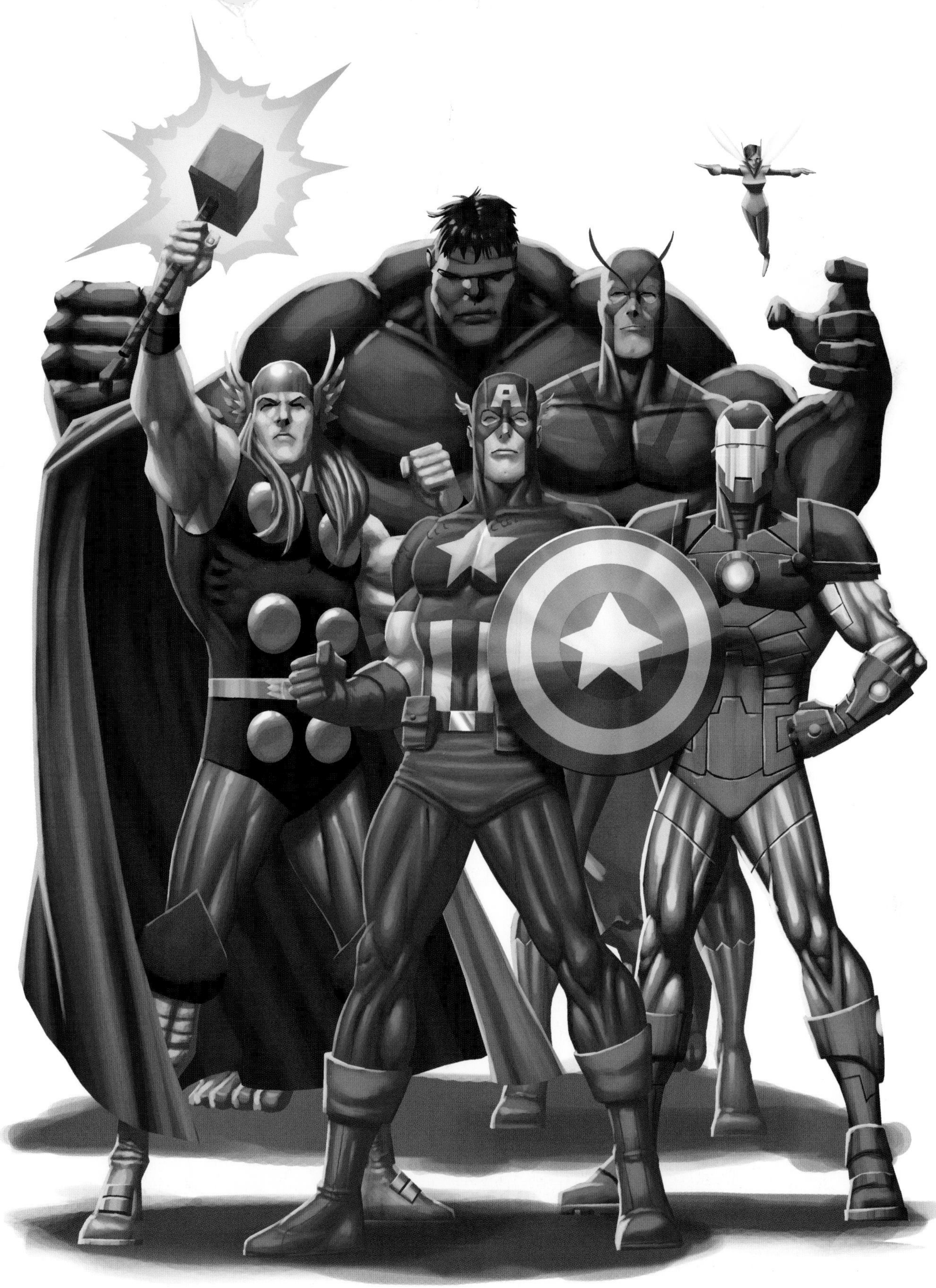
A

. . . and welcomed Captain America back to the world.

Captain America didn't understand what was happening. Iron Man explained that **many years had passed** since the world had last seen Cap. The ice must have kept him in a kind of sleep where he didn't age.

Iron Man brought Captain America to a place in the craft where he could have some time to himself.

Everything Captain America found there was **new** to him.

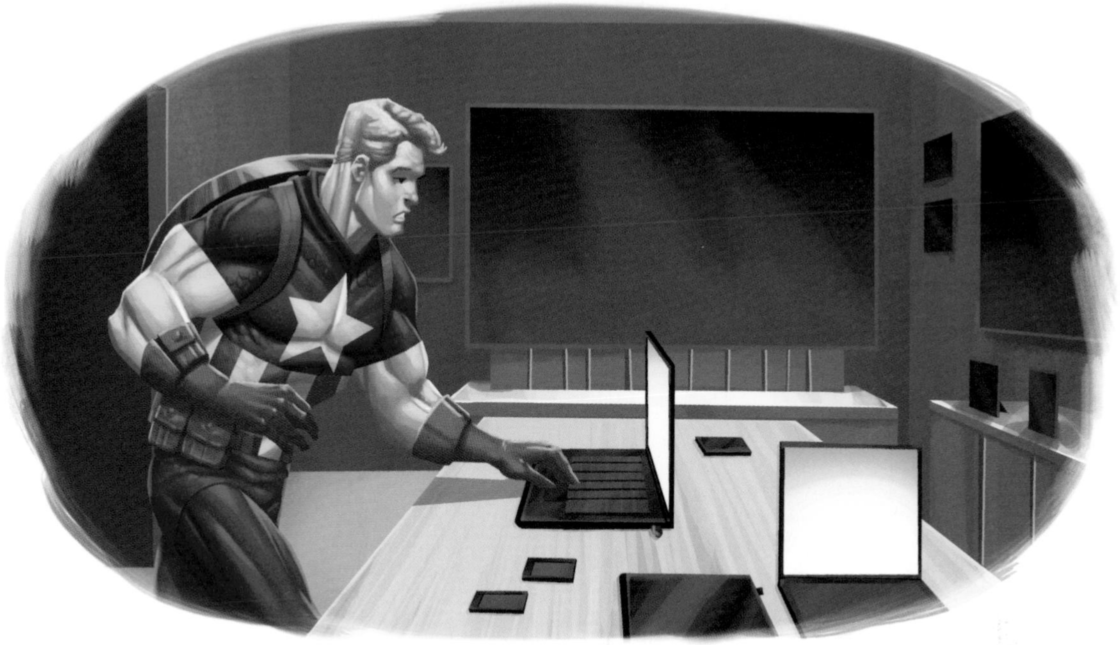

He had no idea how to use any of the things the Avengers had on their ship.

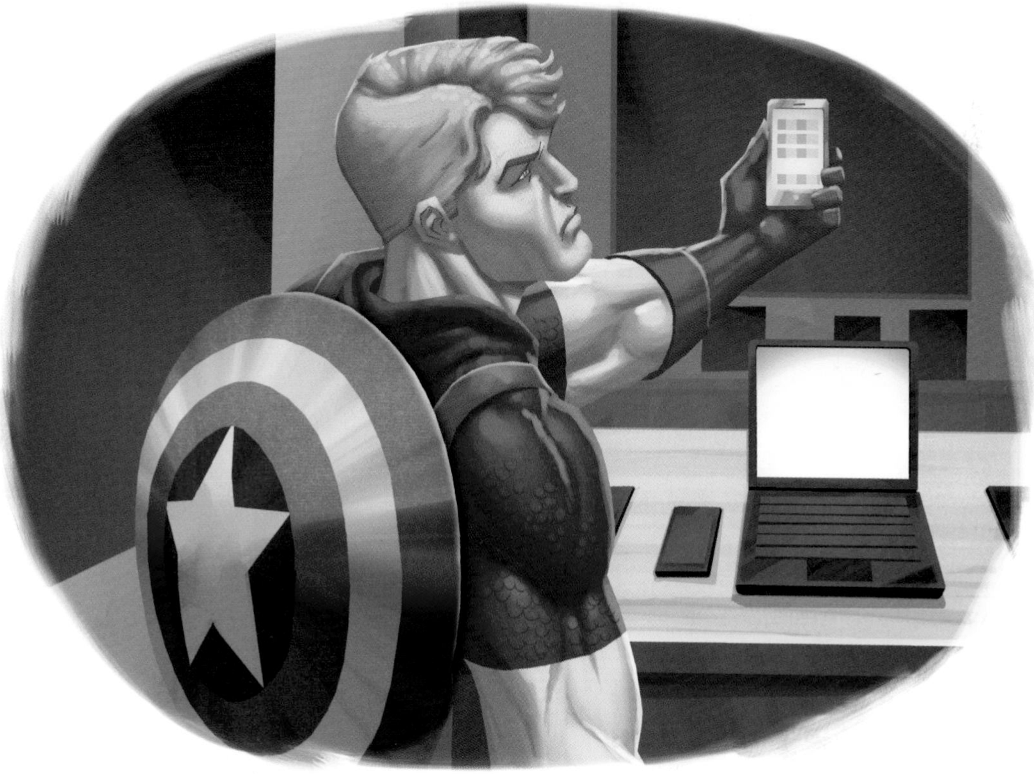

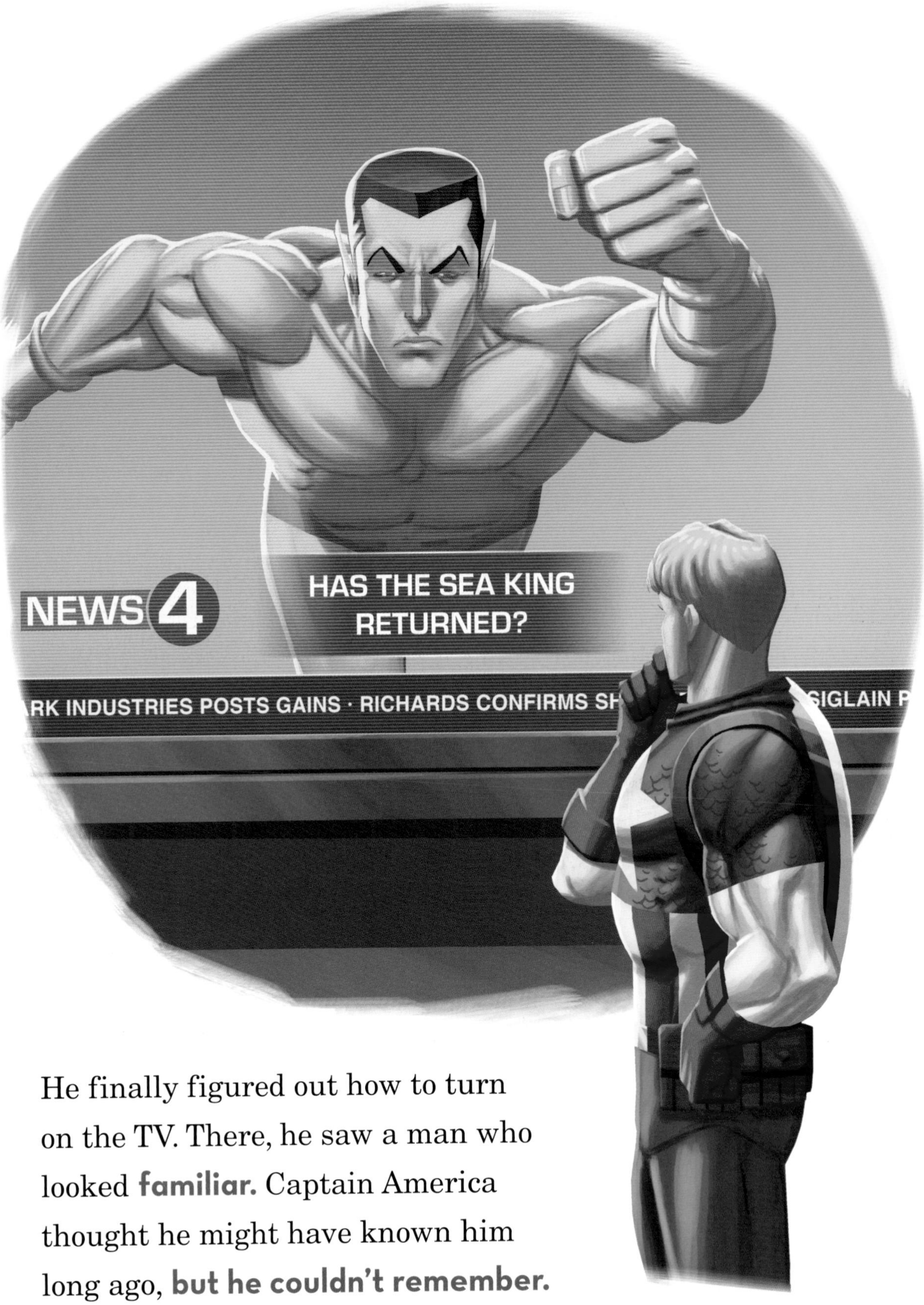
NEWS 4
HAS THE SEA KING RETURNED?
ARK INDUSTRIES POSTS GAINS · RICHARDS CONFIRMS SH

He finally figured out how to turn on the TV. There, he saw a man who looked **familiar.** Captain America thought he might have known him long ago, **but he couldn't remember.**

But before Captain America could wonder more about the man on the screen, **something rocked the craft!**

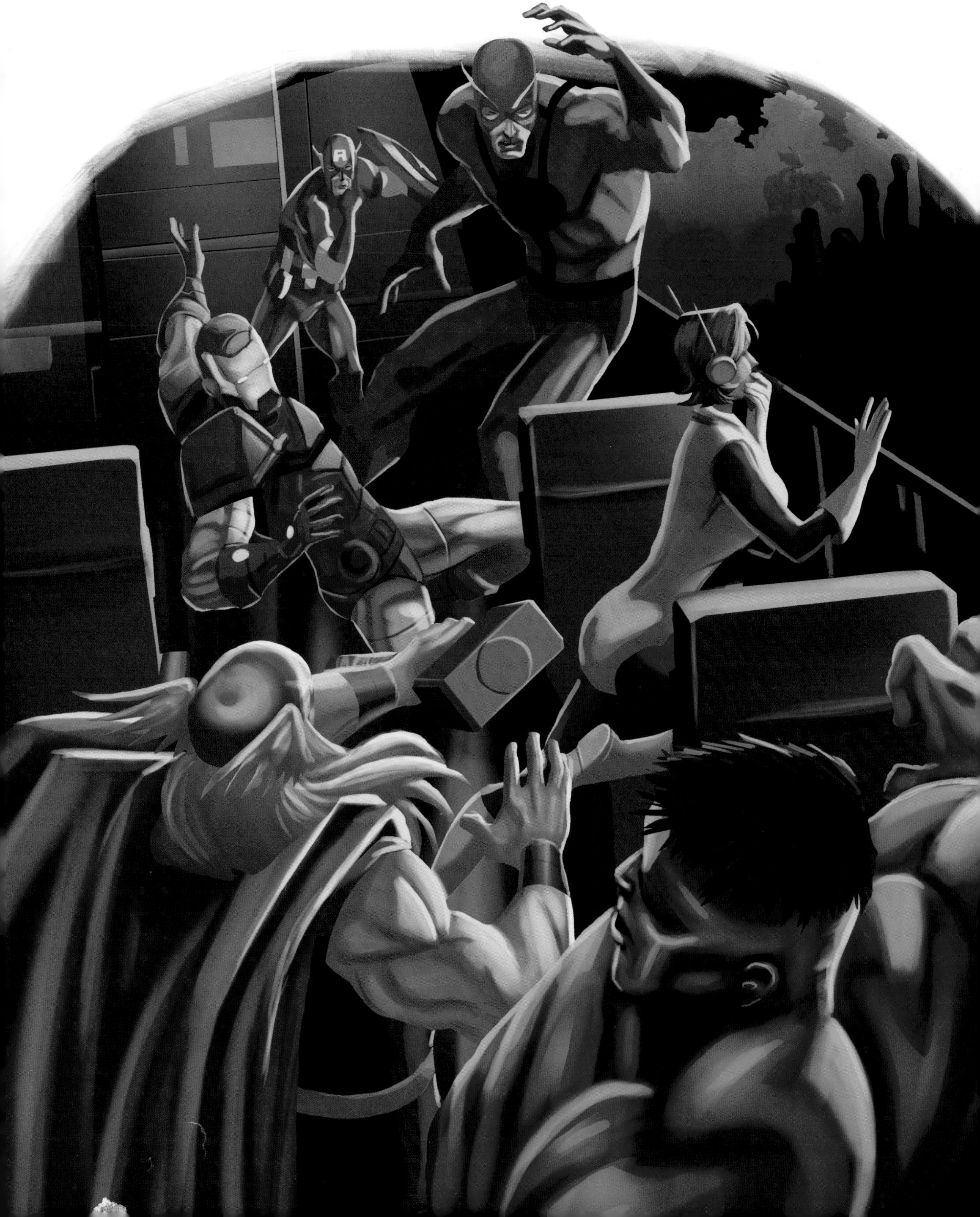

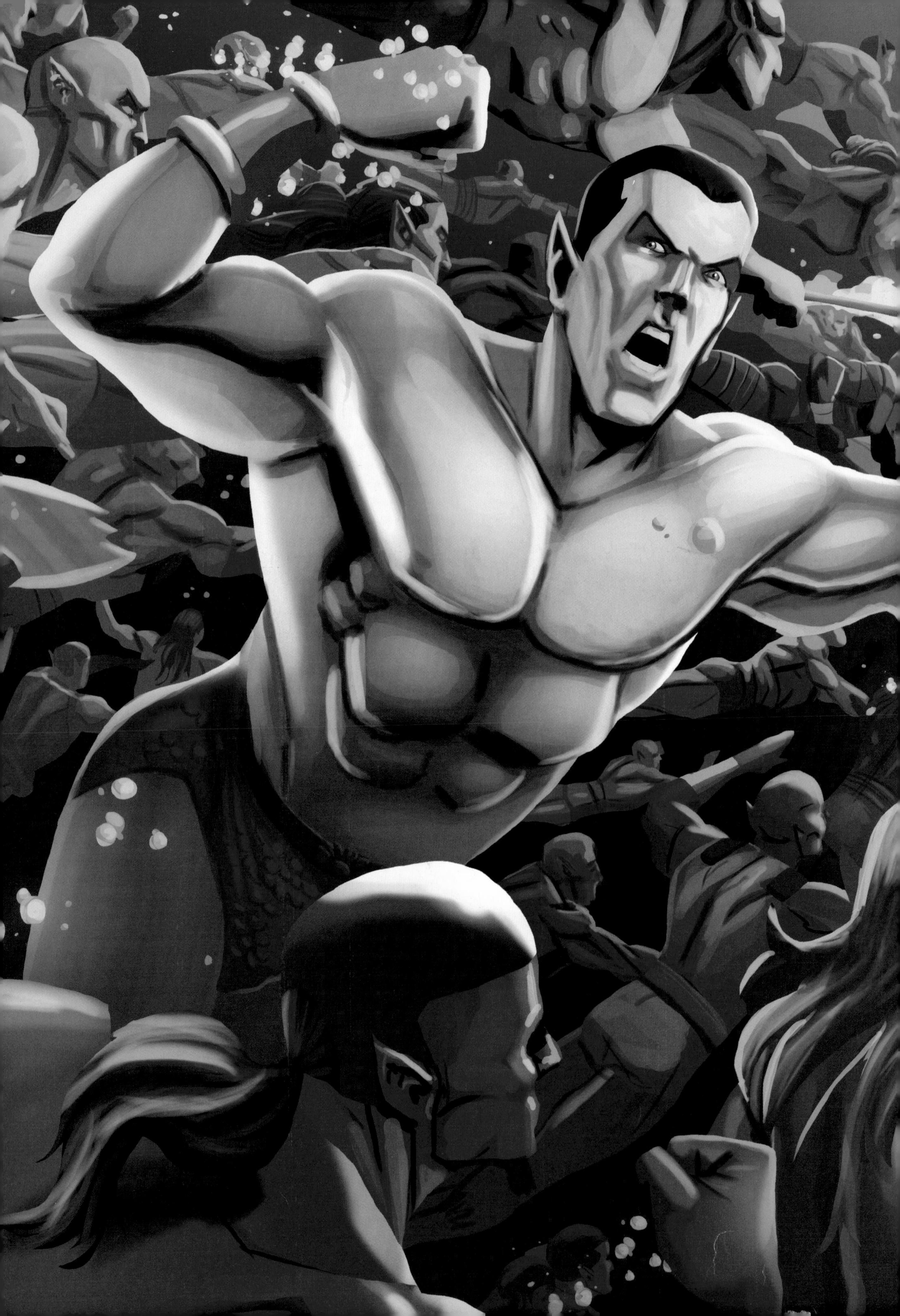

Namor had returned, and he had brought **all the armies of Atlantis** with him!

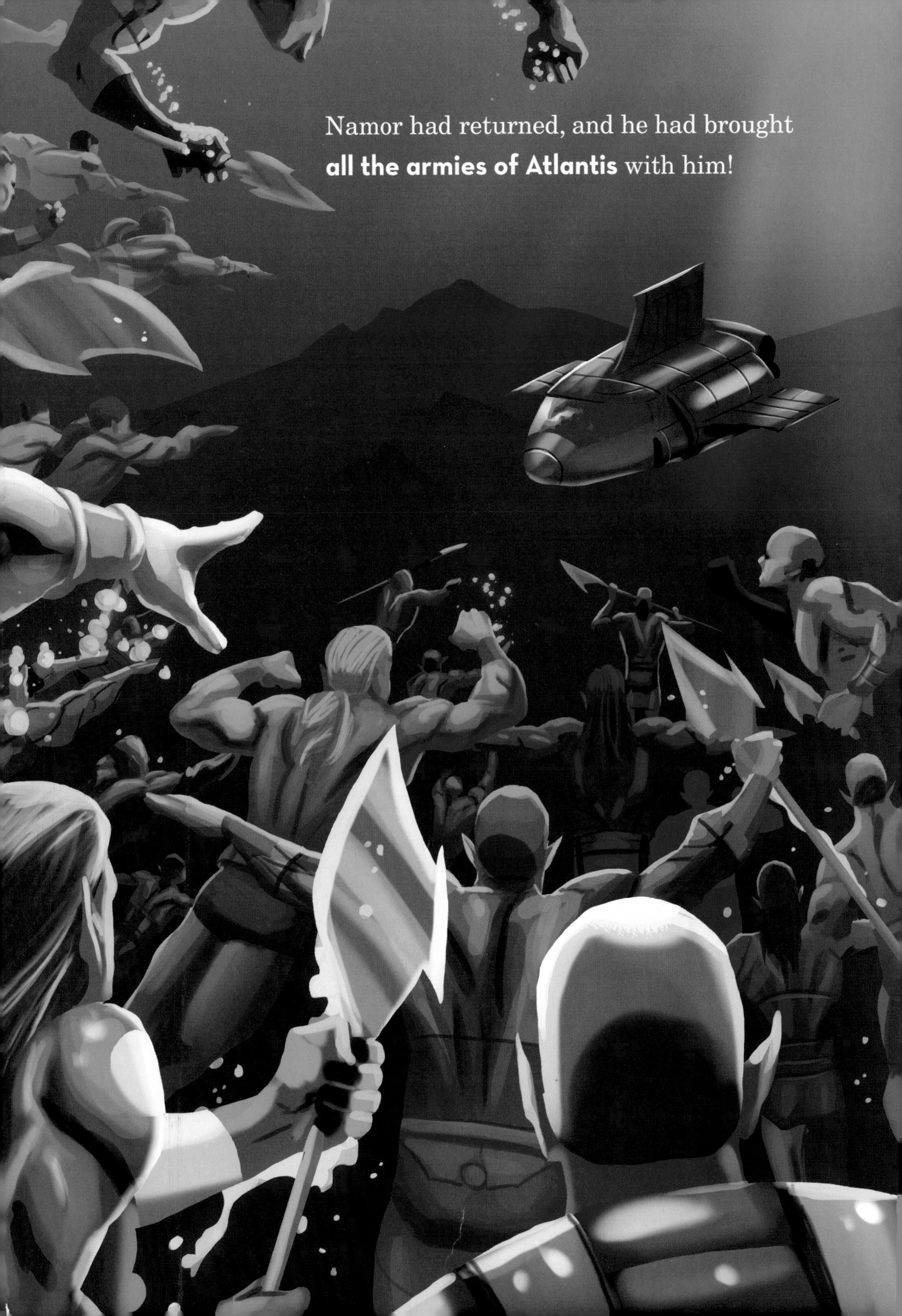

The Avengers rushed onto land, where they knew
the Atlanteans would be weaker.

The Atlantean armies quickly followed.

Thor raised his hammer and cried out for the battle to begin.

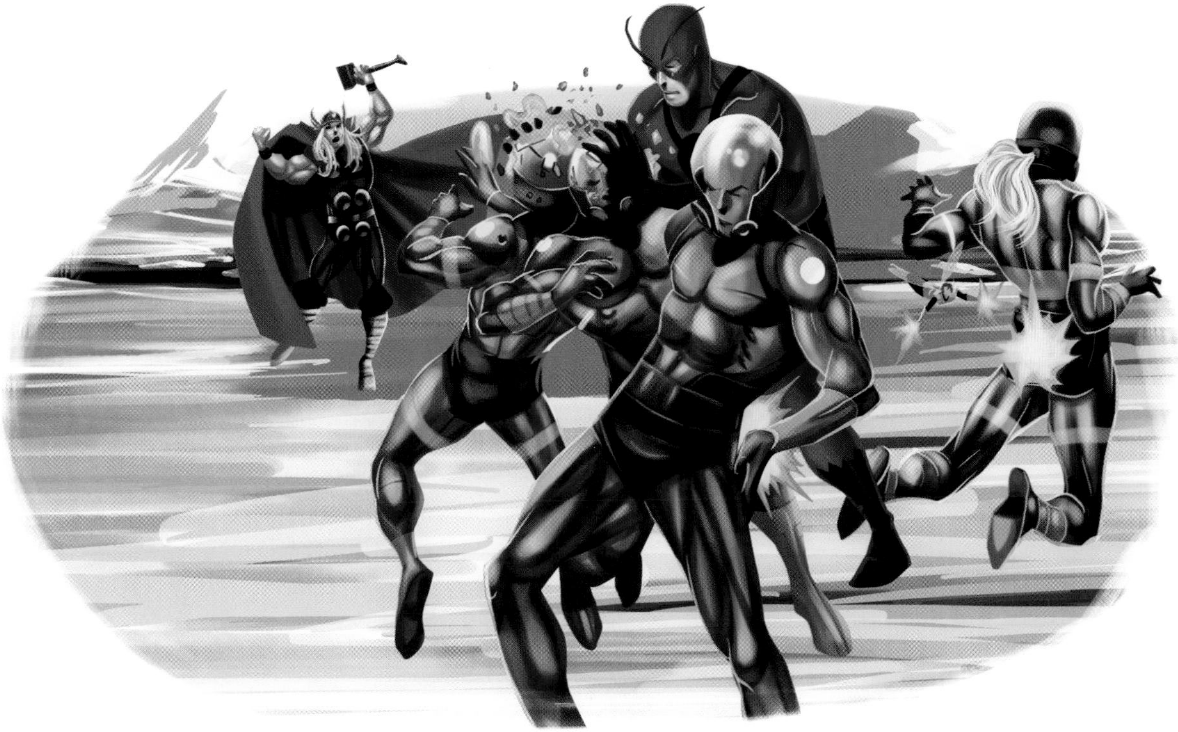

The Avengers fought bravely . . .

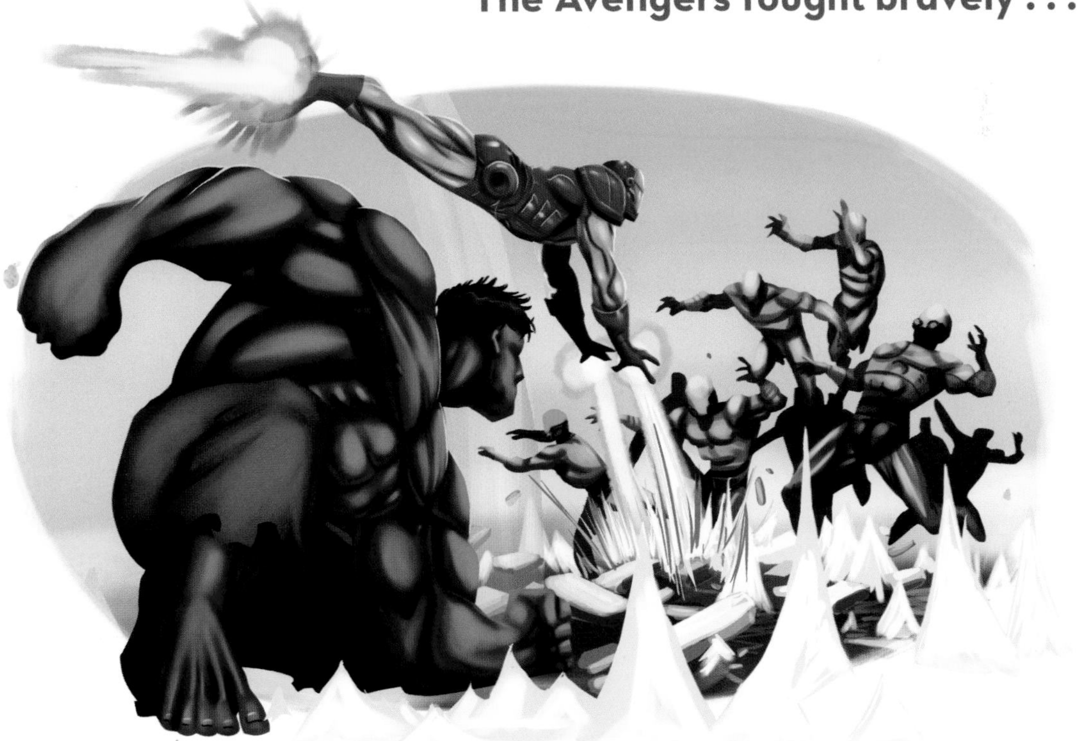

but the Super Heroes were
soon **outnumbered.**

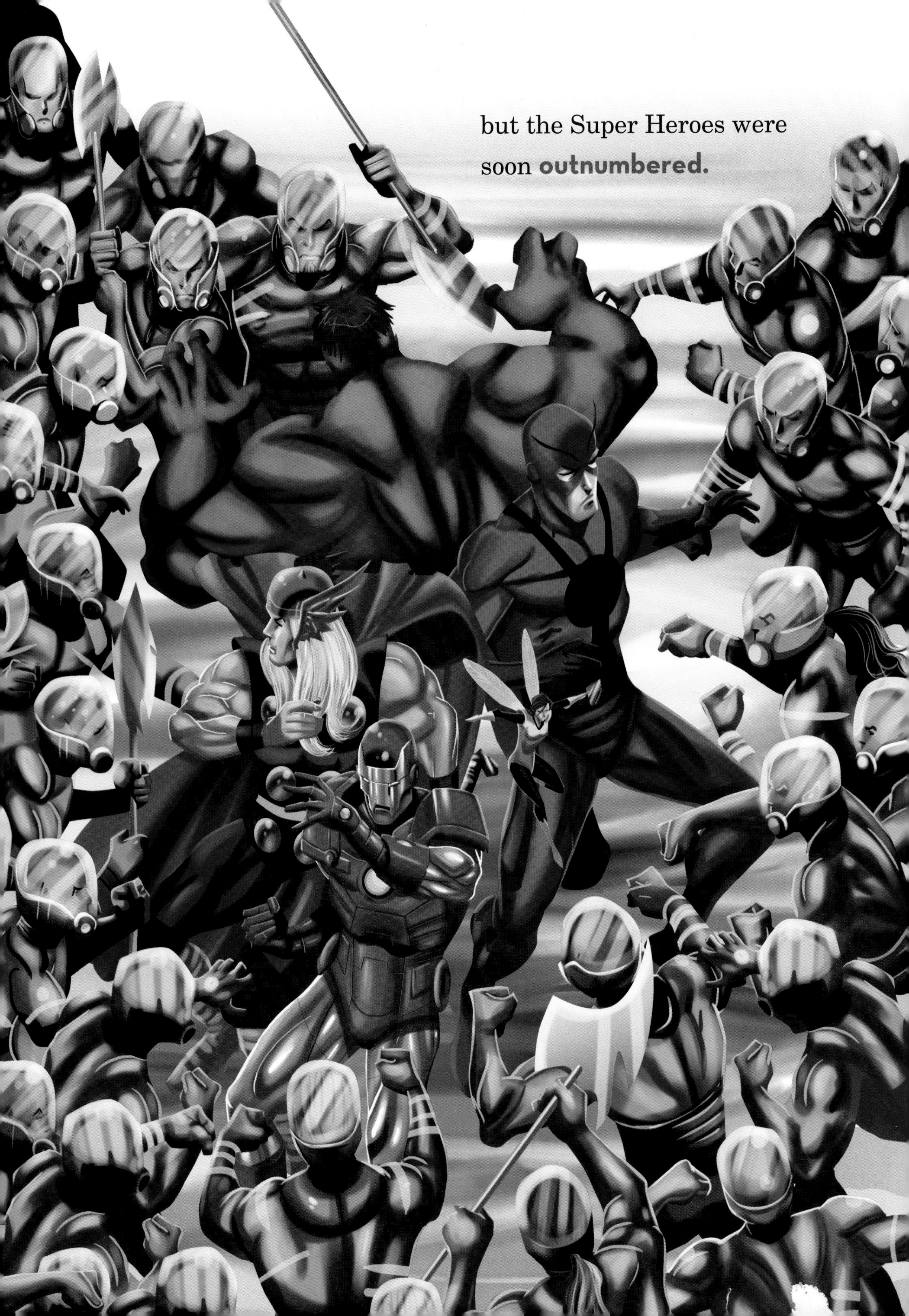

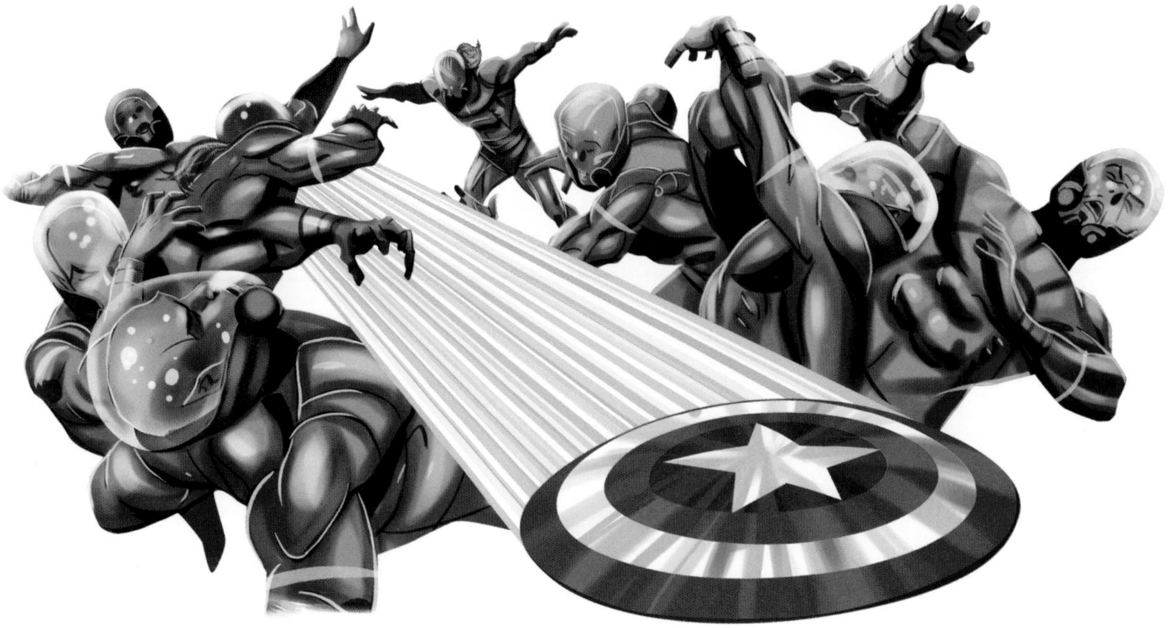

Just then, someone who was not
an Avenger **stepped in.**

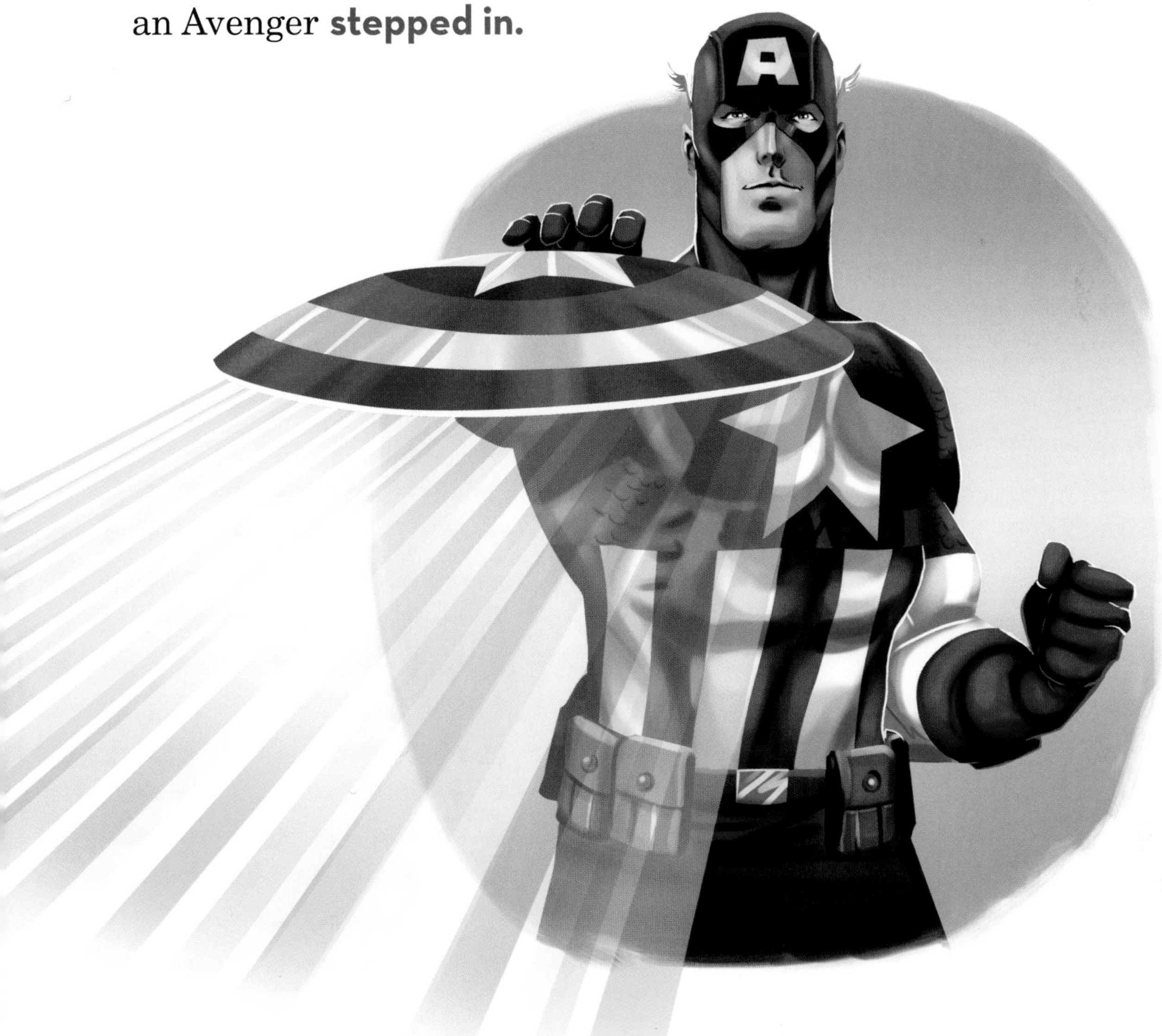

And the tide began to turn.

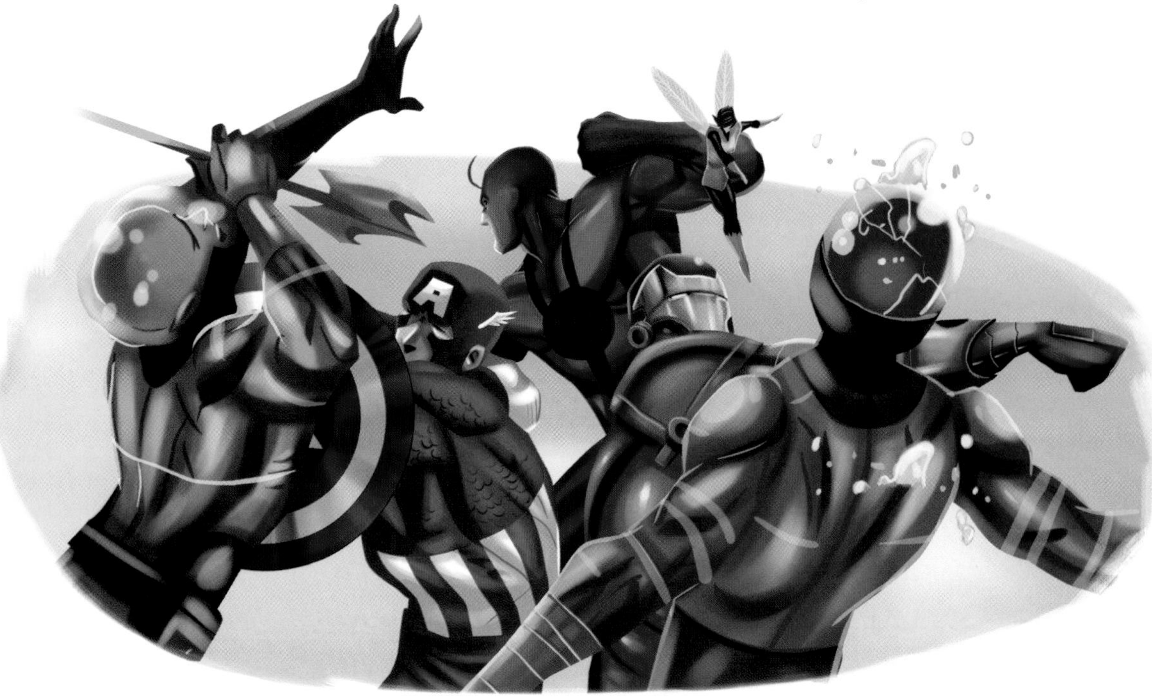

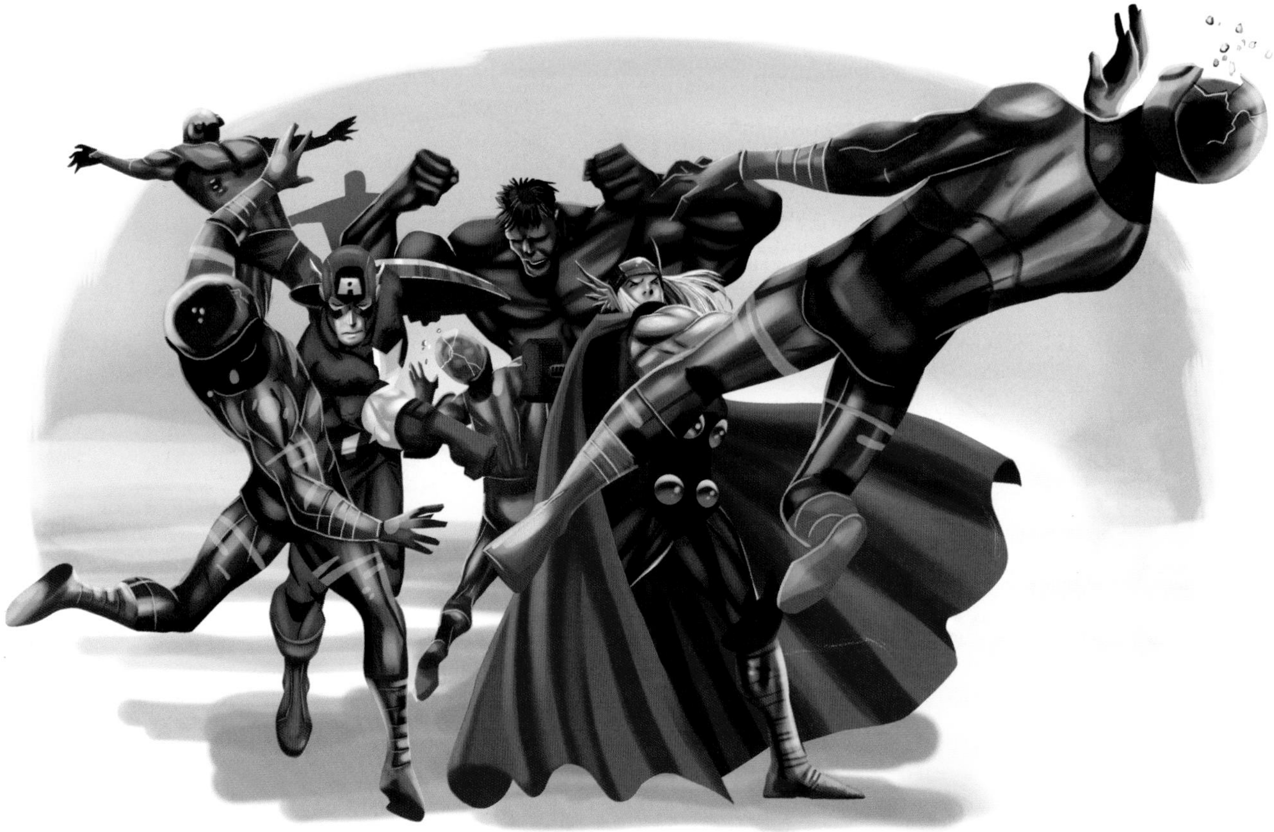

After a long battle, the Avengers—together with
Captain America—drove off Namor and his army.
They had stopped him from waging war on the world!

Neither Cap nor the team could have done it alone.
It was decided to do the only thing that made sense. . . .

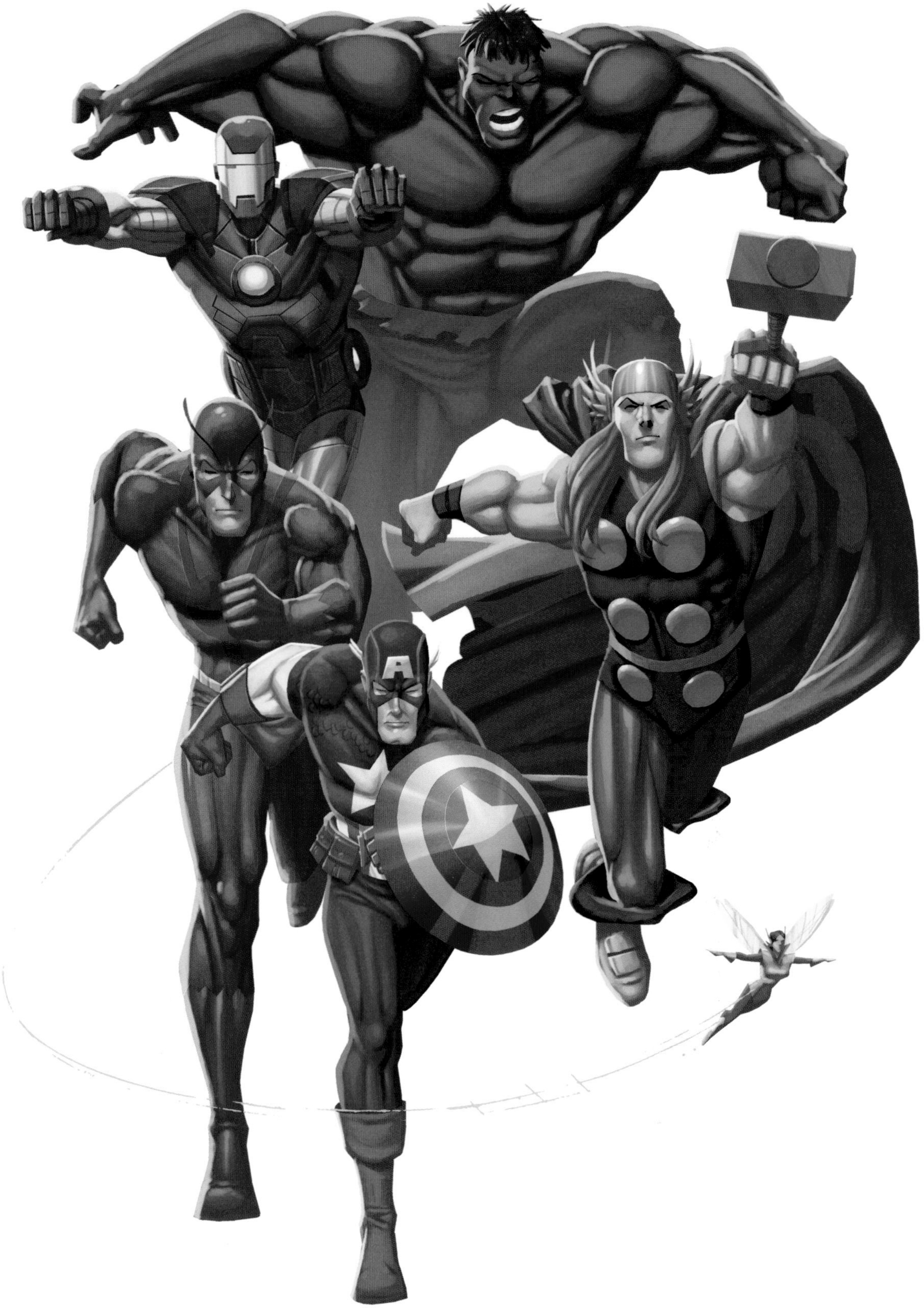

The Courageous Captain America agreed to become
the newest member of the Mighty Avengers!